A fish tale
for our girl ...
Happy Easter 1998
We love you,
Momma + Daddy

LILLIAN'S
FISH

LILLIAN'S FISH

JAMES MENK
ILLUSTRATED BY LOUISA BAUER

PEACHTREE
ATLANTA

A Peachtree Junior Publication

Published by
PEACHTREE PUBLISHERS, LTD.
494 Armour Circle NE
Atlanta, Georgia 30324

Cover illustration by Louisa Bauer
Book design and composition by Loraine M. Balcsik

Manufactured in the United States of America
10 9 8 7 6 5 4 3 2 1
First Edition

Library of Congress Cataloguing-in-Publication Data

Menk, James
      Lillian's fish / James Menk ; illustrated by Louisa Bauer. —1st ed.
      p. cm.— (Lillian's Fish) Summary: When Lillian's pet fish escapes
from her pond and all the other pets band together to search for her, they must
learn to overcome their differences if they are to succeed in their dangerous
mission.
      ISBN 1-56145-158-4
      1. Animals—Juvenile fiction. [1. Animals—Fiction. 2. Adventure and
adventurers—Fiction.] I. Bauer, Louisa, ill. II. Title.
PZ10.3.M52595L1 1997
[Fic]—dc21

                                      97-12331
                                         CIP
                                         AC

To S. P.
(Sorry about the fish!)
—*J. M.*

CONTENTS

A Birthday Party

Long ago and far away lived a little girl named Lillian. Little Lillian lived in a large house with her mother and father, her aunt and uncle, and her seven brothers. Her aunt's name was Alice, her uncle's name was Nat, and her seven brothers were named Tim, Tom, Tod, Tad, Ted, Troy, and William.

At the time of our story Lillian was about to celebrate her sixth birthday. She had celebrated a third birthday and a fourth birthday and a fifth, and would go on to celebrate a seventh birthday and an eighth birthday and even a thirteenth birthday and beyond, but it is her sixth birthday that concerns us. For it was on Lillian's sixth birthday that she received a fish.

It was a tradition in the large house for each child to receive a pet on his or her sixth birthday, and the tradition began this way. When Tim, the oldest boy, was five years old, he found a stray puppy and wanted to keep it. His parents wouldn't allow him to keep it, however. They thought he was much too young to take care of a pet. Tim cried and cried and cried, and his parents, afraid that he might dry up and blow away from so much crying, promised him a puppy on his sixth birthday. And so when his sixth birthday came they had to get him one, because they promised.

(If you ask Tim about the truth of this story he will probably deny it. He isn't five years old any longer and wouldn't own up to so much crying. But it is the truth.)

When Tom turned six he wanted a pet also, and his parents got him a horse, just to be fair. When Tod turned six he got a cat. Tad got a turtle, Ted a bird, Troy a goat, and William a giant spider.

Now Lillian would soon be six, and it was time for her to have a pet. She shouldn't be denied a pet just because she was a girl, should she? She didn't think so, and fortunately, her parents didn't think so either.

To celebrate her sixth birthday Lillian had a party. Her mother and father were there, her aunt and uncle were there, and her seven brothers were there. She was served her favorite foods, which were ham and butter sandwiches (with the crusts left on), and marshmallow soup (a recipe of Lillian's own), and crackers and cream.

After the sandwiches and soup and crackers and cream came the cake, which was six layers high. (Tom and Tim helped carry the cake in because it was so big, and Lillian had to stand on a chair to blow the candles out.) After the cake came dishes of ice cream, with six different flavors in each. Everyone ate as much of the cake and ice cream as they possibly could, and not a crumb more. Uncle Nat fell asleep, Aunt Alice picked up her knitting, and the boys were too full to fight. And then out came the gifts, each wrapped with six ribbons, and each ribbon a different color!

From her mother and father, Lillian received a dress to stay clean in and a pair of rubber boots to get dirty in. From her Aunt Alice, Lillian received a big warm quilt, a quilt that had taken Aunt Alice six months to sew. From her Uncle Nat, Lillian received a necklace of sea shells that Uncle Nat had collected from the days when he sailed the seven seas.

Lillian was so delighted with her new gifts that she carried them up the stairs to her bedroom right away. Her hands were so full with gifts that she didn't even bother with the banister! She put the new quilt on the bed, and the dress on her body, and the boots on her feet, and the necklace around her neck.

Meanwhile, her seven brothers carried in a box from the kitchen and set it down on the dining room table. It was neither a large box nor a small box, but it was quite heavy, as if there were bricks inside it, or barbells, or perhaps Aunt Alice's fruitcake. It was not so heavy that all the boys had to help carry (Tim and Tom and Tod and Tad could have probably managed by themselves), but it was a gift from the seven brothers to their little sister, and none of them wanted to be left out. It was a gift from the seven brothers, and inside it was Lillian's pet.

Then Lillian came downstairs in her dress and boots and necklace and saw the box on the dining room table. She crept up to the box and put her ear to it. A sloshing sound came from inside. The box was filled with water!

"What is this?" asked Lillian.

"It's a present," said Tim.

"For you," said Tom.

"From us," said Tod.

"For your birthday," said Tad.

"For your sixth birthday," said Ted.

"It's a pet," said Troy.

"It's a f—" began William, but Troy managed to shut him up just in time.

"A pet!" said Lillian. "For my sixth birthday! From you! For me! Oh, what kind of pet could this possibly be?"

And with that she tore off the wrappings and the ribbons, lifted up the lid of the box, and looked inside.

4

She tore off the wrappings and the ribbons,
lifted up the lid of the box, and looked inside.

Seven Pets

Lillian was not the only one who wanted to know what kind of pet this could possibly be. There were others, seven others, in fact, who also wished to know, and had been wishing to know for weeks, ever since they found out about Lillian's sixth birthday. These seven others were the seven pets of the seven brothers: the dog, the horse, the cat, the turtle, the bird, the goat, and the spider.

The seven pets of the seven brothers had been very curious about the animal Lillian was going to receive for her sixth birthday. They knew she had a sixth birthday coming up, and they knew she would receive a pet, but what kind of pet could it possibly be?

One day before Lillian's party the seven animals met in the barn. All the animals liked to visit the barn, and they came there often. The dog liked to sleep in the hay, and the cat liked to hunt mice, and the bird liked to perch on the high beams, and the spider liked to spin webs in the eaves. The horse and the goat liked spending time in the barn, of course, because they lived there. The turtle also liked the barn, but he did not visit as often as the others, because it took him a long time to get there and a longer time to get back.

After the turtle had at last arrived and all the animals had assembled in the barn, the horse began the meeting. The horse, because he was the largest, was something of a leader among the animals.

"It is very important that we find out about this new pet," said the horse.

"Why?" asked the goat.

"Well," said the horse, who did not really know the answer to the goat's question, "because good breeding demands it!"

"Oh," said the goat.

That "good breeding demands it" was not the true answer to the goat's question. The true answer to the question of why they must find out about the new pet was buried deep in the horse's heart, and in the hearts of the other animals as well. Perhaps only the dog, in her wisdom, knew this true answer. But the dog was indeed too well bred to speak it.

"I have an idea," said the dog.

"Yes, dog?" said the horse.

"I think one of us should attend little Lillian's birthday party and discover what sort of pet she receives," said the dog.

"An excellent idea!" said the horse. "But which one of us shall it be? I am much too large to fit through the doorway. The turtle is too low to the ground. The spider gives Aunt Alice a fright. The goat, after what happened last time, will never be allowed in the house again. The bird—"

"Pardon me," interrupted the dog. "But I feel it should be either the cat or myself. We both know the house well."

"Quite so," said the horse. "But which one of you shall it be?"

"I nominate the cat," said the dog. "After all, she is allowed on the furniture, and I am not."

"So be it!" said the horse. "Cat, do you accept?"

"Yes," said the cat, who was quite proud of being chosen for such an important job.

"All animals in favor, say 'aye.'"

And so the dog barked, and the cat meowed, and the bird sang, and the horse neighed, and the goat bleated, and the turtle snapped, and the spider, who could not be heard above the din, raised one of his eight little legs, and the cat was elected to attend Lillian's party.

At the party, she sat on the mantelpiece (if you look carefully you can see her) watching as Lillian ripped the ribbons and wrapping from the very last box and lifted off its lid.

An Extraordinary Present

I t's a fish!" Lillian said. "A fish a fish a fish!"

Indeed it was. For inside the heavy box was a big glass tank, and the glass tank was filled with water, and in the water was a fish. It was not an ordinary fish. It was an extraordinary fish. All the colors of the rainbow were on its body, colors that rippled and shimmered as it swam about.

"A fish!" said Lillian. "A beautiful fish! The most beautiful fish I have ever seen! Thank you, Tim! Thank you, Tom! Thank you, Tod! Thank you, Tad, Ted, Troy, and William!"

The seven brothers were only too happy to say "You're welcome." They were glad that Lillian liked the fish, and they gave her some other gifts to go with it. Tim gave her some gravel to cover the bottom of the tank. Tom gave her some plants and rocks to put in the tank for the fish to swim between and around. Tod gave her some fish food, and Tad a book about fish, and Ted a net to catch the fish, and Troy and William a little glass bowl for the fish to travel in.

Lillian caught the fish in the net and placed it gently

in the traveling bowl, which William had filled with water. Then she put the gravel and the rocks and the plants in the big tank and put the fish back in it. The fish swam between and around the plants and rocks. Lillian sprinkled some food on top of the water. The fish came to the surface and ate it. Everyone gathered around the tank to watch the beautiful fish, and no one noticed as the cat leapt down from the mantelpiece and left the room.

The cat found the dog in the kitchen, dozing next to the stove.

"Dog," said the cat, "it's a fish."

"A fish?" said the dog. "And not a puppy, then?"

"Not unless it's a dogfish," said the cat, and slipped through the crack in the kitchen door.

The cat found the spider in the garden, spinning a web.

"Spider," said the cat, "it's a fish."

12

"A fish," said the spider. "A fish, and not another spider?"

"Not a spider, nor a bug of any kind, I think," said the cat.

The cat found the turtle sitting on a rock in the middle of the brook.

"Turtle! Turtle!" called the cat. "It's a fish!"

"What's that?" said the turtle.

"A fish!" said the cat.

"What?" said the turtle.

"Oh, come over here so you can hear me!" said the cat.

"I can't hear you," said the turtle.

"This brook is bubbling a bit too much. Stay right

there and I'll be with you in a moment."

It took more than a moment for the turtle to walk across the slippery rocks to the bank of the brook, but the cat waited patiently, high and dry.

"Now, what was it?" asked the turtle.

"It's a fish," said the cat. "Lillian's pet is a fish."

"A fish," said the turtle. "Well, well. A fish. Are you sure?"

"It swims, but it's not a turtle," said the cat, who was beginning to catch on.

"Well, well."

The cat found the bird perched on a limb of the maple tree.

"Bird!" said the cat. "It's a fish."

"A fish!" said the bird. "A fish! Whoever would have guessed it? A fish. I never! A fish. Isn't that something! A fish. Cat?"

"Yes?" said the cat.

"What is a fish?" asked the bird.

"I don't know exactly," said the cat. "But it swims in water, and looks very good to eat."

The cat found the horse and the goat in the pasture

behind the barn. The horse was munching on some grass, and the goat was butting an empty barrel that happened to be in his way.

"It's a fish," said the cat.

The horse stopped munching and the goat stopped butting.

"Fish?" said the horse.

"Fish?" echoed the goat.

"Fish, did you say?" asked the horse.

"Fish, did you—?" began the goat, but the cat interrupted.

"Fish," said the cat. "Neither horse, nor goat, nor dog, nor spider. Not a turtle, not a bird, not even a

15

cat. A fish. Lillian's fish."

"Insurmountable!" said the horse, which was a word the horse had picked up from the show-jumping circuit, and not at all the right word to use about a new pet fish. But the occasion demanded he use a complicated word, and "insurmountable" was all he could think of on such short notice.

"Insurmountable," said the horse.

"Me too," said the goat.

A Strange Disappearance

Lillian's birthday was in May. As the spring went on and turned into summer, the weather warmed and she began to spend more time out of doors. Lillian loved her pet fish so much that often she would take it with her when she went outside, carrying it about in its small traveling bowl.

Her brother Tad noticed this, and decided to create a surprise for his little sister and her beautiful little fish. Tad liked to play in the brook that ran behind the great house and on through the meadow. On sunny days he would be down there all day, getting wet up to his knees and muddy up to his elbows. He built dams and bridges, and floated toy boats, and placed flat rocks in the water for the turtle to sit on. He put rocks in the brook to create rapids, and took rocks out to make pools.

In the first week of July, Tad spent five days in a row down at the brook, working from after breakfast until just before dinner and sometimes not even taking a break for lunch. He wouldn't tell anyone what he was up to, except to say that it was a secret, and could he bring the shovel down to the brook tomorrow if he promised to bring it right back?

In the middle of the fifth day Tad finished his surprise. He came up to the house, wiped his wet feet on the kitchen mat, and went up to his sister's bedroom and knocked on the door. Lillian was taking a nap under Aunt Alice's quilt.

"Lillian," said Tad. "Come down to the brook. I have something to show you."

"What is it?" asked Lillian, a little cross. "I was having such pleasant dreams." (It is quite all right to become cross with your brothers if there are seven of them and only one of you.)

"Please come down," said Tad. "And bring your fish."

With the mention of the fish, curiosity overcame crossness, and Lillian got out of bed and went down to the brook to see what Tad had done.

What Tad had built was more than just a dam or a bridge or a flat place for the turtle to sit. What Tad had built was something else entirely. A small channel of water branched off the brook and spilled into a small hollow in the meadow, creating a shallow pool. At the end of the pool opposite the channel was a small rock

Lillian put her beautiful fish in Tad's pool.

dam, which kept the water in the pool from running out. Below the dam was another channel that returned the overflow from the dam back to the brook.

"It's very nice," said Lillian, "but what's it for?"

"It's for your fish!" said Tad. "It's a place for your beautiful fish to swim."

"Oh," said Lillian. "How wonderful! But won't the stream mind?"

"No," said Tad. "The water comes from the stream, fills the pool, spills over the dam, and goes right back to the stream."

"Oh," said Lillian.

So Lillian put her beautiful fish in Tad's pool.

The fish liked the pool very much. She liked swimming up and down its length, feeling the cool stream water on her back and belly and fins and tail. She liked to swim among the rocks and pebbles that covered the bottom of the pool. She liked to lie in wait in the shadows of the pool and suck up unsuspecting insects that dawdled on the water. But most of all, the fish liked to leap high into the air with a flick of her tail and land with a big splash on the water.

Every sunny day Lillian would bring the fish down to the pool to swim. She would bring the fish down in the morning and pick her up in the afternoon, before it got too dark.

Every day in the pool the little fish got a little stronger, a little bolder, and a little less little. She explored every inch of the pool. Some days, if she was feeling especially bold, the little fish would swim up the channel against the current until she came to the brook proper. Some days the little fish would poke her brightly colored head around the corner of the channel and into the brook, and then with a flick of her colorful tail, race back down into the pool. But most days the little fish spent her time leaping high into the air and landing with a big splash on the water.

The other animals would often come down to the pool to visit the fish. They could not speak to the fish, except when the turtle was there to translate, but they liked to watch the fish swim. The fish was indeed very beautiful. All the colors of the rainbow were on her body, colors that seemed to ripple and shimmer as she moved about.

The fish liked to swim in front of the animals, too. She considered them friends and would leap high into the air and turn somersaults to say so.

Of all the animals, perhaps the cat visited the fish

most often. The cat loved to lie on her belly a good, safe distance from the water and watch the fish. She was curious about any creature that could live its whole life in—shudder to think of it—all that wet stuff! (After all, even the turtle spent time on dry land!)

And the cat liked to watch the fish move. Cats are attracted to all small things that move rapidly about, like mice and flies and rolling balls of yarn, and this cat was no exception. This cat loved to watch the fish swim back and forth and back and forth and back and forth. The cat found that watching the fish increased her appetite immensely, and after she left the pool she was always very hungry.

One August day the cat went down to the water to visit the fish. The fish was practicing somersaults and was very glad to have an audience. She had managed to turn two somersaults in the air, and now she was going to try for three! How lucky it was that the cat would be there to see it!

So the cat sat down by the edge of the pool and watched the fish turn somersaults. The fish began from the end of the pool and swam with all her might. Then she leapt into the air, did two somersaults, and landed with a splash.

"Very impressive," said the cat. "I'd like to see the turtle do that!"

The second time the fish began her swim halfway up the channel. She gathered even more speed this time, and leapt even higher, and managed to do two and a half somersaults. The splash was so big that the water almost hit the cat!

"Very, very impressive," said the cat. "But you had better be careful, little fish, for you almost landed on the stone dam that time."

The fish could not hear the cat, of course, because she was underwater. She was all the way at the beginning of the channel, and from there she began her swim. This time she swam faster and leapt higher than any time before. She turned one, two, and then three somersaults!

The cat shut her eyes, fearful of the splash of water that would surely come. She shut her eyes and waited, but no splash came. Then the cat heard a distant splash that seemed to come from down the stream.

Slowly the cat opened her eyes and looked about. The fish was nowhere to be seen. The cat crept to the very edge of the water and looked in. But the fish was not there. The little fish had disappeared!

The Cat in Court

The disappearance of the fish caused much conster- nation. "Consternation" was the word the horse used, anyway, and for once he was quite correct. Consternation means fear, and there was plenty of fear that the little fish might never be found.

There was consternation in the great house. Uncle Nat and Aunt Alice, Tim, Tom, Tod, Tad, Ted, Troy, and William, and their mom and dad were all filled with consternation. But the greatest consternation and the greatest grief belonged to Lillian. She had lost the only pet she ever had, and she was very sad.

In the evening, when the house was quiet, you could hear Lillian crying and sobbing, saying, "Oh, my fish! My beautiful lost little fish!" It made everyone very sad to hear this, and sadder still to see the empty tank in which the fish used to swim. Tim, Tom, Tod, Tad, Ted, Troy, and William were so sad that they walked about on tiptoe, and not a dish nor a pane of glass nor a stick of furniture was broken by them for three whole days.

There was consternation in the barn also. The seven animals had grown fond of the beautiful little fish and missed her very much. They were very sad that she had disappeared. But there was another fear the animals felt now that the fish was missing. It was the same fear they had felt before the fish arrived, a fear that lay buried deep in their hearts.

Because of that fear the animals decided to do something, and what they did was bring the cat to trial. The cat had been the last one to see the fish alive and swimming, and therefore they held her partly responsible for the fish's disappearance. The smaller animals, the bird and the spider especially, believed that the cat was entirely to blame.

The bird went so far as to accuse the cat of—it was too horrible to even think of!—swallowing the fish whole. The other animals did not really believe the bird's accusation, but they were still angry with the cat. The cat was the first to report that the fish was missing, and no one likes the bearer of bad news.

The barn served as a courtroom, and it was there that the cat was put on trial. She had to sit beneath an overturned crate, like any common prisoner. The horse was the judge of the trial, and his stall served as the judge's bench. The bird was the prosecutor (she argued against the cat). The dog was the defense attorney (she argued for the cat). The goat, the spider, and the turtle were spectators (a necessary part of any courtroom drama). All the animals except the cat were members of the jury. They would vote on the cat's fate.

"We are here to determine the guilt or innocence of the cat regarding the sudden disappearance of the little fish," began the horse.

"Guilty! Innocent!" cried the spectators, who weren't quite sure what guilt and innocence were and had to have the horse explain it to them.

"How do you plead, cat?" asked the horse. "Guilty or not guilty?"

But the cat, who was furious about having to sit beneath an overturned crate, only hissed at the horse and would not answer the question. The dog had to answer for her.

"Not guilty," said the dog.

The bird spoke first. She repeated the point that the cat had been the last creature to see the fish. Then she called a surprise witness, and that surprise witness was the bird herself. As a witness, the bird recounted the day the fish had first arrived and what the cat had said on that day.

"I asked the cat what a fish was," said the bird,

The barn served as a courtroom,
and it was there that the cat was put on trial.

"and what did you reply, cat?"

But the cat only hissed at the bird.

"The cat replied," continued the bird, "that she didn't know what a fish was, but that it swims in water, and..." and here the bird paused, "that the fish looked very good to eat!"

The spectators all gasped, and the horse had to bang a hoof against the stall to call the court to order.

"Isn't that true, cat?" asked the bird.

"Hsssssssssssss!" said the cat.

"Guilty! Guilty!" cried the spectators, and the horse had to bang his hoof again to call the court to order. When all was calm, the dog began the cat's defense.

The dog was an excellent speaker. She said that although the cat had been seen down by the fish pool, it did not mean that the cat had eaten the fish. The cat, said the dog, was deathly afraid of water. This was a well-known fact, she said, and she called the turtle to the witness stand to say so.

"How could the cat have eaten the fish if the cat was afraid to get too close to the water in the pool?" asked the dog.

All of this impressed the spectators very much, and they began to shout, "Innocent! Innocent!"

29

"Order in the barn!" said the horse. "The jury will now vote."

The jury voted. The horse, the turtle, and the dog voted "not guilty." The bird, the spider, and the goat voted "guilty." It was a tie. The dog recommended letting the cat go free. The bird recommended tying a bell about the cat's neck. Even though he was judge, the horse could not decide what to do.

Up until now the cat had kept silent. She was a very proud animal, and she refused to take the trial seriously. But when the bird suggested tying a bell around her neck she began to worry. The mice would hear that bell from a long way off, and she would never be able to catch one again!

"Horse, dog, bird, members of the jury," said the cat. "May I say something?"

"You may," said the horse, who still had not decided what to do.

"I did not eat the fish," said the cat. "But I know some of you do not believe me. I believe that the fish, on her last leap in the pool, landed back in the water beyond the stone dam and was washed downstream. And we must get the fish back. Do you know why?"

The dog knew why, but she said nothing.

"Why?" asked the horse.

"Because if we do not get the fish back," said the cat, "the little girl may get another pet. She may get a new pet. And this new pet may well be another horse or another dog or another goat or another bird or another turtle or another spider or another cat!"

This was the secret fear buried deep in the hearts of the animals. This was the true reason why the animals had wanted to know what Lillian's pet would be. The cat had discovered this on the day she attended Lillian's party.

The animals had been very happy when they heard that Lillian's pet was a fish. A fish is not a dog, is not a cat, is not a horse, is not a spider, is not a turtle, is not a bird, and is not a goat. If Lillian's pet had been a dog, then the dog would no longer be the only dog. If Lillian's pet had been a horse, then the horse would no longer be the only horse. If Lillian's pet had been a bird, then the bird would no longer be the only bird.

The animals were very much afraid of the idea of a new pet. They were afraid that they would no longer get the love and attention they deserved if they were not one of a kind. After all, everyone knows how much love and attention a brand new puppy or a brand new

31

kitten gets. The bird wanted to be the only bird at the great house. The goat wanted to be the only goat. The cat wanted to be the only cat. In a home filled with so many creatures, human and animal alike, it helps to be one of a kind.

The cat's words hit home. No one wanted Lillian to get a new pet. The dog could have pointed out that Lillian's new pet might be another fish, but she didn't. She kept silent.

"What shall we do then, cat?" asked the horse.

"Go find the fish," said the cat. "Go downstream and get the fish back!"

This seemed the answer to all the animals' problems. It was an answer to the cat's problem, also. If the fish could be found, then the cat would be proven innocent, and no bell would hang around her neck.

"The cat is right," said the horse. "We must go find the fish."

"But what about the cat?" asked the bird. "Guilty or innocent?"

"If the cat is guilty," said the horse, "we cannot let her go unpunished. But if the cat is innocent, it would be terribly cruel to hang a bell about her neck. Therefore, until we have found the fish and returned it to the pool, the cat shall wear a collar about her neck with no bell attached!"

All the animals thought this a very wise decision. All except the cat of course, but a collar without a bell was much better than a collar with one, and so it would have to do.

In the corner of the barn was an old leather collar that the dog had worn when she was a puppy, and with the help of the spider and the bird, it was fastened around the cat's neck. It was an awful experience for the cat to have the bird walking all over her back, and when it was over she shook her head and slunk out of the barn without even a flick of her tail.

On the Path

After the trial, the animals spent the day getting ready for their trip. Only a few of them had been downstream and knew what the land there would be like. And no one knew how far downstream they would have to travel before they found the fish.

The bird believed the fish would not be found downstream at all. She believed the fish would be found inside the cat's belly. Nevertheless, she made preparations for the journey. She gathered sticks and twigs to close up the entrance to her nest so that squirrels and weasels and starlings would not invade it while she was gone. (It was not really necessary for the bird to leave her nest. With her swift wings she could fly back to it at any time, no matter how far the animals on the ground might walk. But she felt it was best for all to keep together.)

The turtle did not need to block up the entrance to his house. He carried his house with him wherever he went. Instead, he spent his time talking to the few creatures that lived in the brook this far upstream (a crayfish, two minnows, and a salamander), trying to get some clue as to where the fish might have gone.

The spider spent his time catching flies and wrapping them up in little bags of spider silk. This way he could bring them along on the trip. Who knew if he would have the time to spin webs along the way? And even if he could spin them, who knew if there were any flies downstream to catch? And even if there were flies to catch, who knew what they would taste like?

The dog was not too worried about food. Something would turn up. It always did. And perhaps she and the cat could go hunting again, like they used to. That would be fun, thought the dog, and so she spent the remainder of the afternoon testing out her nose, making sure it was in working order.

The horse was quite sure there would be plenty for him to eat along the way. Any old sort of hay would do in a pinch. He spent his time pounding his hooves against the side of the barn, to be sure the metal shoes he wore were on good and tight.

The goat, as you may have noticed, looked up to the horse. The horse was the goat's role model, and the goat imitated the horse in every way. So the goat also pounded his hooves against the side of the barn. He did not have any metal shoes on his feet, but he thought it was the proper thing to do before setting off on a journey.

The cat, after trying unsuccessfully to remove the collar from around her neck, curled up in a patch of sunlight and went to sleep. Going on a journey to the outside world was nothing new to her, and she wanted all the other animals to know it.

The next morning, before the sun had even risen above the treetops, the animals gathered in the pasture behind the barn. From the pasture a path began that followed along the brook as it wound its way down into the meadow and beyond. This was the path the animals would follow on the search for the missing fish.

Because the path was narrow in spots, they could not all walk down it side by side. They had to march in order, one animal behind the other. First came the dog, sniffing the ground with her fine, sharp nose. Next came the goat, ready to knock down anything that got in their way. Between the goat's horns, on a few thin threads of spider silk, rode the spider.

Behind the goat and spider walked the horse. The horse kept his wide eyes on the sides of the trail, looking for things the dog couldn't see with her head down. On the horse's back, holding on for dear life, rode the turtle. The turtle kept his eyes on the stream, looking for the lost little fish. He did not see the lost little fish, but he did see some other water creatures, and he asked these creatures questions.

Last in line walked the cat. She was in the back to make sure that nothing snuck up on the animals from behind. It is difficult to sneak up on a cat, because they do so much sneaking around themselves.

Above all flew the bird. From up above she had a bird's eye view, which is always very useful. Occasionally she would flutter down and perch on the horse to tell the others what lay ahead or just to pass the time and sing a few bars of song.

All morning and all afternoon the animals walked alongside the stream. By nightfall they were very tired.

The dog, the cat, the goat, and the horse were tired of the rough trail that wandered up steep banks, down slippery hills, under low-hung branches, over gnarled roots, and around hard gray rocks.

The spider was tired of bouncing around in his silken hammock strung between the goat's horns. Occasionally the wind blew the spider off his perch, and he had to climb up the goat's side on one thin silken thread.

The turtle was tired of riding on top of the horse's back, so high above the ground. The average turtle doesn't get off the ground that often, and while this turtle was not an average turtle, he was still somewhat frightened. What was more frightening than riding on top of the horse's back, however, was getting on and

39

off of the horse's back. Whenever there was a water creature to talk to, it was the turtle that did the talking. (The horse liked to speak of the turtle as the animals' "aqua-ambassador.") Talking to a water creature meant coming down off the horse's back, and coming off the horse's back meant being carried between the sharp teeth of the dog. The life of a diplomat was not all the turtle had thought it would be.

Even the bird was tired. She was tired of flying through dense thickets and tall trees. She was tired of having to fly up and come down, fly up and come down, fly up and come down. She was tired of trying to hover above the brook looking for the bright colors of the little lost fish. By the end of the day she was too tired to sing anything but simple, uncomplicated songs.

When evening came, the animals decided to halt for the night. They camped in a small meadow that bordered a bend in the stream. The meadow was a beautiful spot, and there was plenty to eat for all. A large willow tree grew in the middle of the meadow, and under its sheltering branches the animals settled down to listen to the turtle report on what he had learned from the creatures of the brook.

Meanwhile...

Meanwhile, back at the large house, Tom came down to the barn to feed the horse and the goat. He and Troy took turns doing the barn chores, and today it was Tom's turn. He carried a bucket of oats for the horse in one hand and a bucket of vegetable peelings for the goat in the other. In his pocket Tom also carried the three lumps of sugar that he liked to give to the horse for dessert.

But when Tom got to the barn, the horse and goat were nowhere to be found.

They must be in the pasture, Tom thought.

He put the buckets down and walked out the back door of the barn. But the horse and the goat were not in the pasture, either.

Now where could they be? thought Tom. Perhaps they went to the maple grove, to visit the bird and the turtle.

Tom walked over to the maple grove, but the horse and goat were not there. In the maple grove he met his brother Ted, who had come out to give the bird some seed and suet.

"The bird's nest is all blocked up," said Ted. "And I can't find her anywhere."

"I can't find the horse and the goat!" Tom said.

"Let's see if the turtle is on his rock," Ted said.

Tom and Ted walked through the maple grove to where the brook ran, but the turtle was not on his rock.

"No turtle, no bird, no horse, no goat," said Tom.

"Let's tell the others," Ted said, "and see if the spider and the cat and the dog have disappeared."

Tom and Ted told Tim, Tod, Tad, Troy, and William what they had discovered. Tim, Tod, and William went out looking for the dog, the cat, and the spider. But the dog, the cat, and the spider had also disappeared.

"No dog," said Tim.

"No horse," said Tom.

"No cat," said Tod.

"No turtle," said Tad.

"No bird," said Ted.

"No goat," said Troy.

"No spider!" said William.

And, of course, no fish.

The Turtle Reports

Slowly, the turtle climbed on top of one of the large, twisted roots that jutted out from the willow tree. There he waited for the other animals to quiet down. The animals had cheered up greatly after eating, and they were engaging in some after-dinner conversation. The horse called them to attention.

"If we can cease and desist the post-repast repartee," said the horse, "we will now hear the report of the turtle, who with the great skill and dignity fitting a terrapin of his vocation, has interviewed various water creatures regarding the whereabouts and wherewithal of the missing little fish."

"What did he say?" whispered the goat to the dog.

"He said to be quiet," said the dog.

"Oh," said the goat. "Whereabouts and wherewithal. Of course."

"I have spoken to two crayfish, several salamanders, some minnows, and a party of water striders," began the turtle. "Believe me, it hasn't been easy. Those crayfish have accents thicker than March mud, and it takes at least two dozen water striders to spell out words on the water, and they are insects you know, and it is very difficult to get them to understand even the simplest things, no offense intended, spider..."

"None taken," said the spider. "I'm not an insect. I'm an arachnid!"

"Oh," said the turtle, "pardon me, I'm sure."

"Certainly," said the spider.

"In any case," continued the turtle, "we know that the fish has indeed come this way. The salamanders said, 'yes, definitely.' The crayfish said, 'yes, absolutely.' And I am quite sure that the water striders were in the process of spelling 'yes' before the wind came up and blew them downstream. So we are on the right track, or rather, the right brook. And we can be thankful that the fish is such a colorful fish. It is difficult for any creature, even as dull a creature as a crayfish, to forget seeing such a colorful fish."

"How long ago did the fish swim this way, turtle?" asked the dog.

"The last salamander I talked to saw the fish sometime yesterday afternoon," said the turtle.

"We're not too far behind, then," said the horse.

"No," said the turtle. "I think we are doing well."

"What does the stream look like ahead, bird?" asked the dog.

The bird stuck her beak in the air and fluttered her wings, proud to be called upon.

"Downstream from here the water wanders close to the shoulder of the mountain," said the bird. "It winds through a brown field of something, I don't know what. After the brown field it passes into a pine forest. A very large pine forest. I couldn't see the end of it, even from a long way aloft."

"What do you mean aloft?" asked the goat. "Do you mean where the hay is kept?"

"Far up in the sky," said the turtle. "Not a hayloft."

"The hay is far up in the barn," said the goat.

"Never mind," said the turtle.

"What are pines?" asked the spider.

"Are they good to eat?" asked the goat.

"The big green sticky tree next to the well at home is a pine tree," said the dog.

"That isn't good to eat," said the goat.

The cat yawned, flicked her tail, and sat up.

"I've been there once," she said, "into the pines. I didn't stay long. It is dark in the pines, even when the sun is straight overhead. All sorts of creatures come down from the mountain to drink at the stream and wander among the trees."

"In any case," continued the turtle, *"we know
that the fish has indeed come this way."*

Tired as the animals were, these last words caused them to sleep fitfully that night. They had awful nightmares about huge, dark creatures with big fangs and sharp claws. Only the turtle, who always felt at home (because he carried his home with him on his back), slept well.

To the Pines

In the morning long arms of warm sunlight reached through the swaying willow branches and shook the animals awake. Bees buzzed from flower to flower, delivering little packages of pollen. The crickets, who had been up all night drinking dew and carrying on, were sleeping silently in the shadows.

Being awakened by the sun is very pleasant, and doubly so when your bed is under the long, swaying branches of a willow tree. The animals certainly thought so, and their bad dreams of the night before were soon forgotten. This was adventure! To wake up in a place different from the one you woke up in yesterday! And such a beautiful place! And with so many good things to eat!

But as the day wore on and the animals continued on the path beside the stream, some dark, unfriendly looking clouds appeared in the sky and blocked out the sun. After the last bend in the stream a mountain had come into view. The dark clouds gathered around the mountain like catfish around a drainpipe. They rumbled and grumbled and made impolite comments at the blue sky and fair winds that passed by.

The willow grove gave way to a stand of stately oaks, the stand of oaks led into a wildflower meadow, and the wildflower meadow became a rough brown thistle field. This was the brown field the bird had seen from the air the day before. The thistles were at the peak of their prickliness, and they got caught in everything: the horse's mane, the goat's beard, the spider's web, the dog's hair, the cat's fur, and the bird's feathers. Even the turtle was not spared. A thistle worked its way up under the turtle's shell, and it took the spider quite some time to pull it out.

The thistle field seemed endless. And worse, there was nothing to eat in it! The time for the midday meal came and went. The goat ate some thistles, but there were few things the goat wouldn't eat if he was hungry enough.

Because traveling through the thistle field was so uncomfortable, the animals changed their marching order. The horse walked first. He was the tallest, and his long legs could step over the thistles and stomp them flat. Next came the goat, who was the second tallest. After the goat came the dog, and after the dog came the cat.

The stream bent and writhed and twisted its way through the thistle field, as if it too was uncomfortable among the prickly plants. After one particularly sharp bend in the water, the horse came to an abrupt halt. The goat was busy thinking about better ways to eat thistles (in a thistle stew, maybe, or a thistle porridge, perhaps, or in a thistle hash), and he smacked into the hind quarters of the horse. The dog then smacked into the goat, and the cat into the dog. The spider was knocked from her perch between the goat's horns.

"What happened?" asked the spider. "Where are we?"

"The pines," said the horse.

"The pines!" said the bird.

The horse stood in a small clearing, and the other animals gathered around him. The thistle field had ended, and on the other side of the clearing a pine forest began. The pine forest was dark. It was difficult to see very far past the edge of it. Big pine boughs stretched across the water where the stream entered the forest, and it seemed as if the dark forest was swallowing the stream whole.

"M-m-m-maybe we should go back to the willow grove," said the goat.

Just as the goat spoke, lightning flashed and

thunder boomed, and it began to rain.

"M-m-m-maybe we should camp under the willow for one more night," said the spider, "and see if it is sunnier tomorrow."

"M-m-m-maybe we should camp under the willow for two nights," said the bird.

But the horse was not going to be frightened by a bunch of dark trees and a little rain!

"My grandfather once said to me that a cavalry travels on its stomach," said the horse, "and I for one am very hungry."

"Me too," said the turtle.

"And I," said the dog.

"And I," said the spider.

"I suppose I could do with something to eat," said the bird.

"I'm always hungry," said the goat.

"Cat," said the horse, "are there things to eat among the pines?"

The cat, who was busy pulling thistles from her tail, took her time replying.

"Yes," said the cat. "There are plenty of things to eat among the pines. You can't eat the pines themselves, but there are plenty of things for us to eat among them."

So the animals, convinced partly by the bravery of the horse and mostly by the emptiness of their stomachs, entered the dark pine forest. They moved quietly among the sweet-smelling boughs. And it wasn't until all traces of the clearing and the thistle field had disappeared from view that the cat spoke again.

"Yes," she said, "there are plenty of things for us to eat among the pines. Of course, among the pines, there are plenty of things to eat us, too."

The Mysterious Mystery of the Missing Pets

Meanwhile, back at the large house, the seven brothers and little Lillian gathered in the hayloft. They had gathered originally under the big pine tree that grew next to the well, but when it began to rain they moved into the hayloft. The hayloft was Tim, Tom, Tod, Tad, Ted, Troy, and William's favorite place to get in out of the rain. Sometimes they went there even when it wasn't raining.

Lillian liked the hayloft also. What she didn't like was the ladder that led to the loft. The ladder was very tall, and toward the top of it Lillian always had to shut her eyes. How brave her seven brothers were to climb the ladder so easily! she thought.

(Actually, Ted, Troy, and William also shut their eyes when they got to the top of the ladder. They did not tell Lillian this, however. They enjoyed being thought of as brave, and they weren't about to say anything to spoil it.)

After Lillian and her seven brothers climbed the ladder to the loft and each was seated on his or her favorite bale of hay, the discussion began. The subject of the discussion was the mysterious mystery of the missing pets.

"It appears to me..." said Tom, who often talked about how things appeared to him. "It appears to me, and to Tim and Tod as well, that there are two parts to this mysterious mystery of the missing pets."

"Part number one," said Tim, "why did the animals disappear?"

"Part number two," said Tod, "where did the animals disappear to?"

"We must answer these questions if we are to solve the mystery of the missing pets," said Tom.

So Lillian and her brothers sat on their bales of hay and thought about these two questions. All except Troy, that is, who was busy counting something on his fingers. They sat for some time thinking, until finally Ted spoke.

"Kidnapped!" he said. "I think our pets were kidnapped!"

"It could be," said Tim.

"It is possible," said Tom.

"Maybe," said Tod.

So they sat on their bales of hay and thought about

kidnapping. They didn't think long, however, before Tim spoke again.

"It couldn't be," he said.

"It isn't possible," said Tom.

"Maybe not," said Tod.

"Why?" asked Ted.

"No note," said Tim.

"There is always a ransom note when somebody gets kidnapped," said Tom.

"Always," said Tod.

"Oh," said Ted.

So Lillian and her brothers sat on their bales of hay and continued thinking about the mysterious mystery of the missing pets. All except Troy, that is, who had completed his calculations.

"Sixteen!" he shouted.

"Sixteen what?" asked Tom.

"Sixteen parts!" said Troy.

"What are you talking about?" asked Tod.

"Eight animals and two questions," said Troy. "Eight times two equals sixteen. This mysterious mystery has sixteen parts!"

"I think there is a third question," said Tad.

"What's that?" asked Tom.

"The fish disappeared one day," said Tad, "and all the other animals disappeared the very next day. Is the disappearance of the fish connected with the disappearance of the others?"

"Very good question," said Tim.

"We hadn't thought of that," said Tod.

So Lillian and her brothers sat on their bales of hay and thought about this third question. All except Troy, that is, who continued counting on his fingers. They sat thinking for some time, until Ted spoke again.

"Maybe the animals fell down the well," he said.

"Why do you think that?" asked Tim.

"When my pocketknife disappeared, that's where it went," said Ted.

"I don't think the horse could fit down the well," said Tom.

"Twenty-four!" shouted Troy.

"Oh, be quiet, Troy!" said Tom. "We all know how to count."

"I think they went down the well," said Ted.

"I don't think so," said Tim.

"Then where did they go?"

"That is the mystery," said Tim, "and we have to solve it."

*They sat on their bales of hay, trying to solve
the mysterious mystery of the missing pets.*

So they sat on their bales of hay, trying to solve the mysterious mystery of the missing pets. Even Troy began to think about it. Outside, the wind blew, and the lightning flashed, and the thunder rumbled. Inside, Lillian and her seven brothers thought and thought. Outside, the rain stopped, the sun set, and the moon rose. Inside the hayloft the seven brothers and little Lillian sat, thinking and thinking. If their mother had not called them in to dinner, they would probably be sitting there still.

The Dark Forest

Back in the pine forest, the animals walked carefully along the stream. At times the trail was barely visible. It seemed as if whoever had created this trail had drawn it first in pencil and forgotten to trace back over it in ink.

The trail was also very quiet. Most sounds were faint in the cool, dark gloom. But at times the horse would scuff his hoof against a stone and there would sound a sharp *knock!* At other times the horse would scuff his hoof against a stone and there would be a soft *thud.* Sometimes a dead pine branch would fall from a tree with a loud *crack!* and land with a loud *crash!* But from time to time a dead pine branch would fall quietly from a tree and land without a sound. Even the stream, whose constant gurgling and bubbling and rushing had been a comfort, was often silent.

There was something else peculiar about this pine forest. While crossing the thistle field they had seen storm clouds gathering about the mountain. Just before entering the woods, sheets of rain and bolts of lightning and rumbles of thunder had begun to march like soldiers into the valley. But now, under the trees, the animals could not feel any raindrops.

They could see the tops of the pine trees hiss and sway in the strong wind. They could hear the crack and boom of thunder. They could see an occasional dim flash of lightning. They could even smell the clean, bitter smell of rain, but they could not feel any.

Where was all the rain? Only once in a while would a drop make it through the thick canopy of pine branches. Once in a while a drop would land on the wing of the bird, or in the web of the spider, or on the turtle's shell.

The rest of the rain did not drop at all. The rest of

the rain ran down the thick trunks of the trees and collected in dark pools that spread across the path. Pine needles floated in these pools, spinning slowly in the slight current.

And there was one more thing about this pine forest that bothered the animals. It was a thing the animals had no name for, and that made it even more bothersome. It was a thing the animals could not be quite sure of, and that made it frightening.

It was a thing the sharp eyes of the bird could not see. It was a thing the sensitive nose of the dog could not smell. A thing the cat could not hear, the spider could not feel, and the goat could not taste. But it was there. At least, something seemed to be. The horse knew it, and it made the long mane on his neck tingle. The dog knew it, and it made her nose twitch. The cat knew it, and it made her tail flick and fly. The spider and the turtle and the bird knew it. The goat knew it. It made him want to knock something over.

"I thought I saw something in that thornbush," said the bird.

"No," said the cat. "I heard something in those branches."

"I think something pulled my tail," said the horse,

"back where we passed that spruce."

"I think I smell something," said the dog. "Maybe we will find out what it is around this next bend in the trail."

But when they rounded the next bend they found nothing. Only once did they find something. Once, in a muddy section of the trail, they found an unfamiliar paw print. It was a giant paw print. A print almost as large as the ones Uncle Nat made when he went around in his bare feet. It was a very wide print, too, and showed only four toes.

The horse had never seen a print quite like it. The dog had never sniffed a print quite like it.

"There are plenty of things for us to eat among the pines," the cat had said, "and plenty of things to eat us, too."

A Hungry Fellow

E at," said a deep voice.
"Eat," said the deep voice in a dark cave far up the side of the mountain.

"Eat," said the deep voice again. "Yes. That is what I would like to do right now, have a bite or two to eat. Something sweet, or perhaps something sour. Something dry maybe, or something juicy. Something nice and cool I think, or then again maybe something warm. Eat. Yes. I would like very much something to eat. Just a bite or two, or three or four…"

The deep voice and the big body it belonged to moved toward the entrance of the cave. The large nose of the big body of the deep voice sniffed the air. The large stomach of the big body of the deep voice grumbled.

"Hmmmm," said the deep voice. "Where should I go to find some things to eat? Should I go to the mead-ow? No, too far to walk. Should I to the far side of the mountain? No, too much trouble. What about the stream? Perhaps. Am I thirsty? Indeed I am. Then why not the stream? Indeed, why not? And there are sometimes berries to be found there, isn't that true? True it is. Blueberries. Blackberries. Raspberries. Blueberries and blackberries and raspberries. Yes indeed! The stream! I think I shall visit the stream. I think I would like that very much. Perhaps I could find something to nibble on down there. A bite or two, or three or four, or five or six or seven…"

The deep voice continued talking, and the big body it belonged to lumbered on down the mountainside. The large nose of the big body of the deep voice sniffed the air. The large stomach of the big body of the deep voice grumbled. The giant forepaws of the big body cracked fallen branches in two. The giant rear paws of the big body sent enormous stones skittering down the slope.

The big body of the deep voice was that of a bear. He was a very big bear, and at that moment he happened to be very hungry. Of course, he was always very hungry (except in winter, when he was always very sleepy).

You may think it odd that the bear talked to himself, but the bear had no one else to talk to. Every animal, every fish, and every insect ran, swam, or flew away from the bear as fast as their legs, fins, or wings could carry them. Even the branches of the berry bushes seemed to bend away when the bear drew near.

It had been over a month and a half since the bear had said as much as "Hello" to another creature, and that creature was a skunk! If the bear wished to talk at all (and he often did), he had to talk to himself. He didn't think it was such a bad thing to talk to oneself (and it isn't), and who would tell him otherwise?

He wasn't such a bad fellow, as bears go. He could be quite cordial when he wasn't hungry. Of course, he was always very hungry (except in winter, when he was always very sleepy).

The bear was not the only hungry creature in the pine forest. The goat and the horse and the cat and the dog and the spider and the bird and the turtle were also quite hungry. They had skipped lunch, if you recall, and the time for dinner was approaching.

The cat had said there was plenty to eat among the pines, and the cat had not lied. There was small game for the dog, and there were grassy patches for the horse, worms for the bird, and insects for the spider. But the pine forest was a frightening place, and many a fine-looking meal had been passed up because the animals had been too scared to stop along the trail.

It seemed better to move along than to stop and eat, and it seemed best of all to hurry out of these awful pines before evening came! That was the hope in all their hearts.

"I wish we had never come on this awful journey!" said the bird.

"Me too," said the spider.

"Oh, shut up, bird!" said the cat. "You're not helping matters any, chittering away like that!"

"Chittering away!" said the bird. "I don't chitter! And as for you, cat, we wouldn't be in the spot we're in if you hadn't swallowed the fish in the first place!"

This caused the cat's fur to fluff up, and she hissed loudly at the bird.

"Stop it! Both of you!" said the horse. "We all wish we were home right now, sitting down to dinner."

"I'm not the least bit hungry," said the goat, and that was indeed unusual.

"We must keep moving along," said the horse.

But that was easier said than done. Moving along had become increasingly difficult. Earlier the trail had been barely visible. Now at times the trail was not at all visible. Occasionally it would fade away completely, and the dog and her nose would have to scout ahead and find it before they could continue.

Toward evening the trail passed through an area clear of pine trees. In this clear area grass and berry bushes grew. There were blueberry bushes and blackberry bushes and raspberry bushes.

The rain had stopped, and the setting sun came out suddenly from behind a cloud. Orange light filled the little clearing, and the animals among the trees thought that their hopes had come true.

"Look at that light!" said the bird. "It must be the end of the pines!"

The dog went bounding ahead through the brush and into the clearing to see if this was so. She was gone an awfully long time, a whole minute at least, and when she returned she did not bound at all.

"Is it the end?" asked the horse.

"It is the end," said the dog, "but not of the pines. It is the trail that has come to an end. There is no more."

It was only too true. The trail entered the little clearing, bent sharply to the left, plunged down the bank of the stream, and disappeared under the cool, dark water. That the trail might end had never occurred to the animals. It was a thought too horrible to think, and now that it had happened it was too much for the goat to take, and he began to cry.

"Now what shall we do!" he said. "We shall never get out of here! We are lost, lost, lost!"

"Nonsense," said the horse, who was ever the optimist. "It is not we that are lost, but rather the trail that has lost us. We must stop for the night, and this clearing seems as good a place as any. It is pleasant here, and there is plenty to eat for all. Tomorrow is another day. I for one am going to feast on these berries. They look quite palatable."

The berries were indeed very palatable (which is a fancy way of saying tasty and delicious). The animals ate quite a few of them, and after they ate they felt much better. Adventures weren't all bad! Tomorrow was a new day, and all that was needed now was a good night's sleep.

The animals were not the only ones in the forest who found the berries palatable. The bear also found them palatable, although he would never have used such a fancy word to say so. The bear liked the berries so much he began to talk about them as he made his way down the mountainside.

"Berries!" he said. "Berries for my big hungry belly! Raspberries, blueberries, and blackberries! Raspberries, blueberries, and blackberries for a big black bear, and that bear is me! A bushel of berries. Barrels of berries. Billions of berries. Berries for bear, and this bear for berries!"

The big, black, berry-hungry bear moved on down the mountainside on a well-worn path that led from the mouth of his cave down to the stream valley below. He slid and slumped and skidded his way down—on his belly, on his back, and on his great big behind. Thick branches cracked under his giant paws and enormous stones went rumbling and tumbling and booming down the slope.

He slid and slumped and skidded his way down until he came to a fork in the trail, and there the bear stopped. A big old hickory tree grew between the forks in the trail, and on the bark of this tree were two sets of long, deep scratch marks running up and down the wood. The bear sat down on his great big behind.

"Now, what is this?" asked the bear, sniffing at the scratches. "And freshly made, too."

The bear tilted his big black head back and looked up the trunk of the giant hickory. Then the bear turned his big black head to the left and looked down the left fork of the trail. Then the bear turned his big black head to the right and looked down the right fork of the trail.

"Such destruction!" said the bear to himself. "Such misbehavior! Such…such…vandalism! It must be that catamount. That pesky catamount, sharpening his claws on my hickory tree!"

Since the wolves had been driven from the mountain, the catamount was the closest thing the bear had to an enemy. The catamount was not much of an enemy, since he couldn't possibly eat the bear (and eating one another is one way wild things deal with their enemies). The bear could not eat the catamount either. The catamount was always too quick. And although the catamount was not nearly as large as the bear, his claws were just as sharp, if not sharper.

He is always sneaking around, that catamount, thought the bear. And the nerve, the cheek, the gumption! Sharpening his claws on my very own hickory tree!

"I tried to befriend him," said the bear aloud. "I tried to have a civil conversation with him. A conversation between equals, but he would have none of it. He just snarled at me, and hissed at me, and took a swipe at my big black nose with one of his puny paws!"

72

All that the bear said was true. The bear loved good conversation almost as much as eating and sleeping, and sometimes even more. He often tried to speak to the other animals in the woods, if he wasn't particularly hungry. It was a lonely life the bear led, and more often than not, all he wished for was someone to talk to.

So there the bear sat, in the fork in the path by the big hickory, wondering what to do about that rude, pesky catamount. He sat there until the rain came and the rain passed. He sat there until the sun went down and the moon came up.

He sat there on into the night, until suddenly his stomach let out a loud groan. It was a rumbling, mumbling, grumbling groan, and it made the bear remember what it was he had come down the mountain for. He sat up with a start, and with a shout of "Berries!" he slid and slumped and skidded his way down the left fork of the trail.

A Fright in the Night

In the clearing at the path's end, all the animals were asleep. All except the bird, that is. She was nesting in the horse's mane, wide awake.

The bird had very sensitive ears. She had ears so sensitive she could hear a worm crawl. All night long her sensitive ears had been hearing things. She heard crunching sounds and munching sounds and thumping sounds and bumping sounds. She heard snapping sounds and tapping sounds and rapping sounds and slapping sounds. She heard squeaks and peeps and pips and pops. She heard hoots and screams and hollers and howls.

Even with her head tucked under a wing she could hear the awful sounds, and she wished very much to be back home in her safe and comfortable little nest. Adventures! thought the bird. Adventures are fine things when the sun is shining bright and the bees are buzzing around the meadow flowers. But adventures aren't such fine things when they lead a bird into a dark pinewood full of all sorts of horrible who knows what!

And what was that awful sound? An awful crashing

sound! Louder than any sound yet! And getting louder! Whatever it was was coming their way!

"Horse!" said the bird. "Wake up! Wake up! Wake up!"

"I am awake," said the horse. "You have hardly allowed me to be anything but. What is it now?"

"Don't you hear it?" asked the bird. "Don't you hear that awful sound?"

"Hear what?" asked the horse. "All I've heard all night is your constant twittering. I do not hear anything in the least bit—"

And then the horse stopped speaking, because he did hear something. He heard a crashing sound. A smashing, crashing sound. A bashing, smashing, crashing sound and it was coming their way!

One by one the other animals also heard this terrifying sound, and one by one they awoke.

"I smell something awful," whispered the dog.

"I see something awful," whispered the cat. "Something I've never seen before!"

"I feel something awful," whispered the spider.

All the animals felt it then. The turtle felt it inside his leathery shell. The goat felt it in the whiskers of his chin. And then they could hear it! Whatever it was was beginning to speak!

"Berries!" said whatever it was, in a very deep voice. "Soon I shall have my berries! Raspberries, blueberries, and blackberries. Berries for a big black bear! This is the spot. I can smell them now. Berries! First a little drink of water from the stream…"

Great gulping sounds filled the night. It sounded as if the dam on the stock pond had burst and all the water was rushing out.

"…and then a little wade across the water…"

Great splashing sounds filled the night. It sounded as if a whole herd of cattle was crossing the stream.

"…and I shall have my berries!" said whatever it was (and whatever it was was the bear), and it scrambled up the stream bank and into the animals' camp.

Catamounts

When the bear splashed his way across the stream, none of the animals moved a muscle. But when the great dark shape of the bear appeared above the stream bank, the sight was much too much for the goat. He was so frightened he could not help himself, and with head lowered and horns raised, he charged with all his might into the body of the bear. The goat butted the bear so hard that the bear landed with a great big splash back in the middle of the stream.

Frightened even more by his own bravery, the goat scampered around to stand behind the horse.

"What have you done?" asked the horse.

"I couldn't help it," said the goat. "I just could not help it. I was so very scared!"

And the goat began to cry.

"There, there," said the horse. "It's all right."

"And what of the spider?" asked the goat. "The spider was sleeping between my horns!"

"I am all right, goat," said the spider, who crawled out from the goat's ear. "But I must say you gave me a fright."

"You see?" said the horse. "Everything is quite all

The bear had not been scared away,
as his deep voice soon made clear.

right. And perhaps you scared whatever it was away."

But everything was not all right. The bear had not been scared away, as his deep voice soon made clear.

"WHO ARE YOU?" said the bear in his deepest and loudest and most terrible voice. "And what are you, that you would strike me in such a way? I tell you now, unless you taste horrible, I SHALL HAVE TO EAT YOU!"

The animals were silent and very frightened. Finally the horse mustered up the courage to speak.

"We are just a small group, sir," said the horse. "Just a small, harmless group, looking for a little lost fish."

"Are you a catamount?" asked the bear.

"Well," said the horse, who had never heard of any such creature, "one of us is a cat, and I am considered by some to be a mount."

"Then I shall have to eat you!" said the bear. "For I do not like pesky, puny catamounts!"

After these words the bear climbed back up the stream bank and settled his giant body in the animals' camp. The animals moved as far away from the bear as they could, as fast as they could, until their backs pressed against the berry bushes. The bear took his time before speaking again.

"Why, there are quite a few of you, aren't there?" he

81

said. "All the better, for I am very hungry. I am so hungry, I could eat a horse!"

The bear had never seen a horse, much less tasted one, but it was an expression he had picked up from some mockingbirds, and he liked to use it often.

"P-p-p-please, sir," said the horse, "do not eat us. We are really not very good to eat, I'm sure."

Again the bear took his time in speaking.

"That is for me to decide," said the bear. "For I am a bear, and a bear eats WHATEVER HE WISHES!"

And with these last words, the bear, quicker than one would think possible for a creature his size, snatched up the animal closest to him in his gigantic jaws.

A Taste of Turtle

The closest animal happened to be the turtle. His little leathery legs had not carried him very far across the clearing when the bear came back up the bank. It was his unfortunate body that was now caught between the sharp teeth of the bear.

But try as the bear might, he could not crack the turtle's hard shell. He ground away with his big back grinding teeth, but couldn't do it. He pierced and poked with his sharp front fangs, but couldn't do it. He sanded and scraped with his large rough tongue, and still couldn't do it. And then, with a loud "Ptooey!" the bear spat the turtle out.

The turtle turned and tumbled across the clearing, coming to a stop against the dog. No little leathery legs emerged from his lifeless body. No little leathery head poked out of his shut-up shell, and the animals were all very afraid that they would never see him again.

"Do you all taste like that?" asked the bear.

"Why, he is the tenderest and tastiest among us," said the dog, who was very wise.

"Then I am afraid I shall be unable to eat you," said the

bear. "And that is most unfortunate, for I am very hungry."

The bear let out a long sigh and sat back on his great big behind.

"I just can't seem to get a bite to eat today," he said.

The bear sniffed the air with his great big nose, and eyed the animals with his big black eyes.

"I must say you don't smell at all like any cata-mounts I have ever smelled. And you don't look like any catamounts I have ever seen, except for that one over there," he said, pointing a paw at the cat.

The bear let out another deep sigh.

"Whatever shall I do?" said he. "I must have some-thing to eat. Are you absolutely sure that none of you are tasty? Might I try a leg or a tail?"

"I can assure you, sir," said the dog, "that none of us are as sweet and tender as the turtle you just tasted."

"Turtles, eh?" said the bear. "So that's what you are. I've heard about turtles, but I had no idea they came in so many shapes and sizes. I really must get out more."

"Why don't you eat berries?" asked the dog.

The bear sat up.

"Berries!" he said. "Yes! Yes! Beautiful black- and blue- and raspberries! Sweet and lovely! Tender and delicious!"

With one great push of his great hind legs, the bear leapt over the animals and plunged into the berry bushes. The animals, gathering around the lifeless shell of the turtle, could hear the bear crashing and thrashing and tramping about. They heard his giant jaws chomping and chewing and swallowing. They heard him shout, So sweet! chomp chomp So tender! chomp chomp So delicious!

"Is the turtle all right?" asked the spider.

"I don't know," whispered the dog. "Only time will tell. In the meantime, I think it would be a good idea to ask the huge black creature if he has seen the little lost fish."

"Chomp chomp chomp!"

"After he has eaten his fill, of course," said the dog.

"Perhaps the fish is in his belly," whispered the spider, but no one heard him above the noise of the hungry bear.

"I think that is a good idea, dog," said the horse. "After all, he is a rather large creature, and it is well known that large creatures have a proportionally large...abdominal capacity...ahem."

"What does 'abdominal capacity' mean?" whispered the goat.

"I think it's another word for stomach," said the bird.

While the huge berry-hungry bear gorged himself in the bushes, the animals discussed which one of them should ask the bear about the little fish. It was at last proposed to send the bird. The bird was best suited for such a dangerous job, because she could fly away at the first sign of trouble.

The bird did not like the idea at all, and it took some convincing on the horse's part to get her to agree. The horse took the bird aside and explained the gravity of their quest, and how important it was to find the little fish, and how she would be known forever after as the bravest bird in all the land if she would ask the big, black bear about the little lost fish. At last the bird agreed she would go, but only after the bear had eaten his fill of berries.

The animals waited and waited. The big black bear chewed and chomped and swallowed. No signs of life came from the turtle's shell. He lay still, closed up and quiet, in the same spot where the bear had spat him out.

The animals waited and waited. Still the big black bear chewed and chomped and swallowed. At last, when the rising sun had begun to brighten the eastern edge of the forest, the bear chewed his last chew and chomped his last chomp and lay down with a great crash among the berry bushes.

"Hurry, bird!" said the horse, who had been keeping watch. "Hurry! Before he falls asleep!"

The bird took wing and perched on a branch of a berry bush above the reclining form of the giant bear. She was very nervous, but she tried not to show it.

"Oh, great, giant creature," said the bird, "may I ask you a small question?"

The bear gazed up at the bird and let out a huge yawn. His great sharp teeth and enormous tongue were stained blue from all the berries he had eaten.

"Certainly, little flying turtle," said the bear. "I enjoy a little after-dinner conversation. Or is this

after-breakfast conversation? Never mind. Ask away."

"Have you heard or seen anything of a brightly colored fish that swam through this way?" asked the bird.

"A brightly colored fish?" asked the bear.

"Yes, sir," said the bird.

"Speckled, like a trout?"

"Not speckled, sir," said the bird. "She has broad bands of color, like the rainbow. Colors that seem to shift and shimmer as she swims about."

"A rainbow trout, do you mean?" asked the bear.

"Not a trout of any kind, I think," said the bird.

"Hmmmm," said the bear. "I'm afraid I cannot help you. I have not seen any such fish. I suggest you ask a trout, though. They know the most about what is in the water and what isn't."

"Where might we find a trout?" asked the bird.

"Follow this stream down a little way," said the bear, "until it meets up with the creek that comes down off the mountain. After the two waters meet there is a small set of rapids. The trout usually spend their summers in those rapids."

"Thank you very much!" said the bird. "And good day to you!"

"Good day to you, little flying turtle!" said the bear.

"Stop by here again if you should return this way. I always enjoy a good talk."

What the Trout Had to Say

With the bird's news the animals once again prepared to set off. Although they were very tired, having had only half a night's sleep, they were quite happy to put some distance between themselves and the big black bear.

Before they set off, however, the animals tried to revive the lifeless body of the turtle. They called his name and knocked on his shell, but no little leathery legs emerged from his motionless body, and no little leathery head poked out of his shut-up shell. At a loss for what to do, they attached the turtle to the horse's back with some sticky strands of spider silk, and off they went into the woods.

There was no longer any trail to follow, so the animals had to make their own trail, and they had to keep the stream in sight at all times. It was rough going. Thickets of young spruce trees grew in this part of the forest, and their supple, spiny branches whipped the animals in the face and along their flanks.

The young spruce trees grew so close together that it was impossible to see very far ahead. Deep muddy rivulets suddenly appeared underfoot, and there was nothing to do but splash in and out of them. It took a long time to travel even a few feet, and soon the animals became discouraged.

"This is what I call bushwhacking!" said the horse.

"Don't you mean tree whacking?" asked the goat. "It's trees that are whacking me, not bushes."

"It makes no difference whether it's trees or not," said the horse. "It's called bushwhacking!"

"Oh," said the goat.

"I wish we were back among those berry bushes," said the bird.

"Not with that giant turtle-eating creature back there, you don't," said the dog.

"I suppose you're right," said the bird. "But I can't help wondering if the giant creature might have lied to us about where the trout are. Perhaps he was mad because he couldn't eat us, and he wanted us to get lost in the woods."

But the bear had not lied. Bears don't lie. They have no need for it. Eventually the animals came to the place the bear had described, where the other creek came down off the mountain, and soon after that they heard the sound of water rushing through rapids.

92

Next to the rapids was a long, thin, sandy beach. The animals stopped on the beach to rest and think about what to do next. "Gathering their wits," the horse called it. They were bloody and muddy and hungry and tired, but happy to be out of the horrible spruce thickets.

"We must see what we can do about getting the turtle out of his shell," said the cat, "or else we shall never be able to speak to a trout."

"Quite right," said the horse.

"Spider," said the dog, "see if you can find a way inside the turtle's home and tell him that we are in need of his diplomatic expertise."

The turtle was removed from the horse's back and placed on the sandy bank. The spider wandered over every inch of the shut-up shell, but could not find an opening large enough for even a creature of his small size to crawl through.

The bird tried pecking on the shell with her sharp beak, but this produced no reaction. The turtle lay quiet and still on the sand.

The goat suggested that the horse sit on the turtle and squeeze him out of his shell. The horse said that would not do. So they stood (and sat and perched) silently on the bank, thinking of a way to get the turtle out of his shell. They stood (and sat and perched) until they heard a voice say:

"I knew there would be streams in heaven, but I never knew they would be as rocky as this."

"Turtle!" all the animals shouted, for it was the turtle who had spoken.

"I guess I'm not in heaven," said the turtle, and shut himself back up in his shell.

The bird fluttered to a perch atop the turtle's shell and said, "Turtle! You must come out! You must! You have to talk to the trout so that they can tell us where the little lost fish is. Only you can do it, turtle, only you!"

"It is all right now, turtle," said the horse. "The giant beast is far away. There is no one here to eat you."

The turtle's head came halfway out of his shell, and only his eyes and nose could be seen.

"Are you sure?" asked the turtle.

"Yes," said the horse.

"Absolutely sure?" asked the turtle.

"Absolutely," said the horse.

"Positively?" asked the turtle.

"Absolutely positively," said the horse.

And with that, the turtle came out of his shell, leathery legs and all.

It took some time for the turtle to find a trout to talk to. Trout are shy and reclusive and somewhat unsociable. But they are also very smart fish. The turtle was sure that if he could talk to a trout he would receive some news of the little lost fish.

There is a wise old saying, If you wish to speak to a trout, come bearing gifts. So the spider spread his web and soon caught a dozen flies. These he bundled up and gave to the turtle. The turtle took them out into the stream and dropped them one by one into the deep dark pools.

The first few flies floated on down the stream unmolested. Then, in an especially dark and deep pool, one fly went under in a large splash. The turtle dropped the remaining flies into this pool, and in splash after splash they all disappeared. When all were gone the turtle spoke.

"Oh, wise and noble trout," the turtle said, "I wish to have a word with you."

A sleek brown head poked out of the pool.

"Who is it that tosses tasty little flies into my pool?" asked the sleek brown head.

"It is I," said the turtle.

"I've seen her," said the trout.
"Strangest-looking fish I ever saw."

"A turtle, eh?" said the trout. "*Chrysemys picta*, if I'm not mistaken."

"Yes, sir," said the turtle.

"Not from around these parts, are you?" asked the trout.

"No," said the turtle. "I'm from far upstream, on the west branch."

"Never been over that way myself," said the trout. "Water's too warm for my taste. What can I do for you?"

"We are searching for a little lost fish. A brightly colored little fish, with colors that shift and shimmer as she—"

"I've seen her!" said the trout. "That I have. Came through this way about two days ago. Strangest-looking fish I ever saw. Stuck out like a bullhead in a bass nest. A beautiful fish, though, I must say. And quite delicate, too. 'A little lost fish,' she said she was, and I believed her. The water is too rough around here for a fish of that nature. I told her to keep on going, down to where the water smooths out. That's the best place for a delicate fish like that. She had no place in wild water like this."

"How far away is this smooth water, sir?" asked the turtle.

"Down before the marsh the water is smooth," said

97

the trout, "and past that it gets even smoother. It's about half a day's swim for me, taking it easy. Can't say how long it would take for you."

"Thank you, Mr. Trout," said the turtle. "You have been a great help."

"Don't mention it," said the trout. "I hope you find her. If you do, tell her old Brookie says hello."

"I will!" said the turtle, but the trout had already disappeared beneath the water.

The other animals were encouraged by the turtle's news. Things were finally looking up. And to make matters better, the dog found a trail at the far end of the sandy bank. This trail followed closely the course of the water, and everyone agreed that any path at all was better than tramping through spruce thickets.

Before they got under way, however, one slight problem had to be solved. While the turtle was perfectly willing to ride on the horse's back, he was no longer willing to be carried to and fro between the dog's sharp teeth.

"Quite understandable," the horse said.

"And quite a problem, I'm afraid," said the turtle.

"Why don't you try riding on my back?" asked the cat. "If I sit down you should be able to climb on without any help."

So the cat sat down, and the turtle climbed onto the cat's back. But the cat's back was much too narrow for the turtle's wide, boxy body, and it was very difficult for him to stay on.

"Why don't you try riding on my back?" asked the dog. "If I sit down you should be able to climb on."

So the dog sat down, and the turtle walked from the cat's back to the dog's back. But the dog's back was still too narrow for the turtle's boxy body, and he kept slipping this way and that.

"How about me?" asked the goat.

So the goat sat down, and the turtle climbed from the dog's back to the goat's back. The goat's back was wide enough for the turtle, and the problem seemed to be solved. But then the goat began to walk in the way that goats will walk, in hops and leaps and bounds. The turtle had to hang on to the goat's hair by his teeth.

"This won't do!" said the turtle. "Perhaps you should just leave me here, and I will meet you on your return."

"We can't do that," said the bird. "You must come. No one else can speak to the river creatures."

"I suppose you're right, bird," said the turtle. "But at the pace I walk, it will be winter before we find the fish!"

"I have it!" said the horse. "Just stand where you are, goat, stand where you are."

So the horse got down on his belly, and the turtle walked from the goat's back to the horse's back, the horse stood up, and they all set off down the path.

The dog was first in line, sniffing the ground with her fine nose. Next came the goat (with the spider between his horns), ready to knock down anything that got in their way. Then came the horse with the turtle, and last in line walked the cat. Above all flew the bird, coming down occasionally to tell the others what lay ahead, or just to pass the time of day and sing a song.

Because the Fish Can't Fly

Meanwhile, back at the large house, Tim, Tom, Tod, Tad, Ted, Troy, William, and Lillian met in the hayloft. They were there to resume their discussion about the mysterious mystery of the missing pets. Lunch had just been finished and dinner was a long way off, and they had all afternoon to solve the mystery. When everyone was there, and all had found seats on their favorite bales of hay, Tim began the meeting.

"Another day has passed," he said. "The animals still have not returned. We must solve this mystery."

"At yesterday's meeting," Tom said, "We reduced the mystery to three questions."

"These questions are," said Tod, "number one, why did the animals disappear? Number two, where did the animals disappear to? And number three, is the disappearance of the fish connected with the disappearance of the other animals?"

Ted counted the questions off on his fingers.

"Does anyone have any answers to these?" asked Tim.

"Me and Lillian do!" shouted William. He and

Lillian shared the same bale of hay, and until then both of them had kept quiet.

"You mean 'Lillian and I do,'" said Tom.

"What do you mean?" said William. "You weren't there! Lillian and me met in her room last night, and we solved the mysterious mystery!"

"Lillian and I," said Tom.

"It was me!" said William.

"Never mind," said Tom. "Go ahead."

"Lillian and me figured that if you answer the last question first, then all the other questions answer themselves," said William.

"What do you mean?" asked Tod.

"And then number one is the same as number three!" said William.

"Huh?" said Ted.

"The fish got lost, and the other animals went to look for her," said William. "And that's the *why,* number one and number three! And the *where* is wherever the fish might be!"

"That rhymed," whispered Lillian to William.

"That's impossible!" said Ted. "You've made one equal three, and it can't be done."

"Hold on a minute," said Tim, "the little ones

may have something there."

William and Lillian made faces. They hated being called "the little ones."

"If the other animals did indeed go to look for the little fish, that narrows down where they might be," Tim said.

"Why?" asked Troy.

"Because the fish can't fly, and she can't walk either," said Tim. "The fish can only swim. Wherever the fish is, she's in water. And if the other pets are looking for her, then they must be in the water, too, or close to it!"

"It does make sense," said Tod. "The fish disappeared one day, and all the others disappeared the very next day. Perhaps they did go look for the little lost fish."

"And we should go look for them!" said Troy.

"The most logical place to begin looking is the brook that runs through the meadow," said Tim. "It's the closest body of water around, it's easy to follow downstream, and keep in mind that it connects to the pool in which the fish was last seen."

"Let's go!" said Troy.

"Not so fast," said Tad. "There is another question

that we have to answer."

"What's that?" said Ted.

"Mom and Dad know that the little fish is lost, right Lillian?" asked Tad.

"Right," said Lillian.

"But has anyone told them that the other pets are missing? I know I haven't," Tad said.

"I haven't," said Tim.

"Not me," said Tom.

"Nor I," said Tod.

"Nope," said Ted.

"Nuh-uh," said Troy.

And William and Lillian just shook their heads.

"We can't keep the secret forever," said Tad. "Pretty soon they'll discover that all the pets are missing. When they do discover that, they will want to know why we didn't tell them, and then we'll all be in trouble."

"Maybe they already know," said Tom.

"If they do," said Tod, "we're already in trouble."

"So who is going to tell them?" asked Tad.

"Perhaps we should draw straws," said Tim.

"No way!" said Ted. "I always get the short one."

"Somebody has to tell them," said Tom.

"Not me," said Tod.

"Me neither," said Troy.

"I think Tom should tell them," said William.

"Why me?" asked Tom.

"Because your pet is the horse," said William, "and he's biggest, so he's missing the most."

"That's ridiculous," said Tom. "I think you should tell them."

"How come?" asked William.

"Because you're the littlest," said Tom, "and they won't punish you as much."

"Lillian is littler," said William.

"Am not," said Lillian.

"Are too," said William.

"Lillian can't tell them," said Tim. "Mom and Dad already know her pet is missing."

Lillian stuck her tongue out at William, and he stuck his tongue out at her.

"Somebody has to tell them," said Tom.

"Not me," said Tod.

"Me neither," said Troy.

"I think Tad should tell them," said Ted.

"Why me?" asked Tad.

"It was your idea," said Ted.

And so it went. They argued on into the afternoon about who should tell their mom and dad about the missing pets. Each was afraid that he would be the one chosen to break the horrible news. One by one, Tim, Tom, Tod, Tad, Ted, and Troy snuck off down the ladder, until only William and Lillian remained in the hayloft. They were arguing about who was littler.

"You are," William said.

"Am not," said Lillian.

"Are too."

Into the Marsh

When the sun had set and the long shadow of the mountain had stretched out to meet the rising moon, the animals were at last out of the dark forest. It had been a long day. The path they picked up at the sandy bank that brought them out of the woods was even stranger than the path that had brought them in.

It seemed to have a will of its own. It threaded through the trees without rhyme or reason, turning to the left here, turning to the right there, narrowing down to a ribbon's width in one spot, branching off into five directions at once in another. If not for the talented nose of the dog, they might never have found the way out.

This peculiar path also passed through some very frightening scenery. It tunneled through a briar patch, whose inch-long thorns pricked and pecked at the animals' flesh. It crept through a damp and gloomy grove of rotting hardwoods, where vines and creepers of every sort hung from the leafless branches.

Most horrible of all, the path passed through the site of a recent forest fire. This area was covered with acre  after acre of blackened stumps and the blackened skeletons of once proud pines. Not a creature stirred among the ashes, and not a sound could be heard except the wind sighing through the charred bones of the burnt trees. It seemed as if even the trees themselves were not safe in a wood like this.

But that was the worst part of the path. Past that desolate place, saplings grew beside the path and ferns covered the forest floor. The trees thinned out and then disappeared completely, and the animals found themselves on a wide grassy  plain that bordered the suddenly still waters of the wide stream.

108

It was none too soon. The animals were too tired to talk and barely had the energy to eat. The cat and dog paired off to hunt small game, and when they returned, they promptly fell asleep. The bird and the spider ate insects until they could eat no more, and they too fell asleep. The turtle, on his way back from a feast at the stream, fell asleep in midstride and did not return to camp until morning. The horse and the goat nodded off where they sat, with half-chewed tufts of grass still between their teeth.

In the morning, the animals took a closer look at their surroundings. The stream was wide enough to be called a river, and on the opposite bank of the river, the dark pinewood continued as far as the eye could see. The animals were very glad to be on this bank, where the sun shone and the breeze blew the grass about in bright green waves. Grasshoppers hopped about above the blades, and in the river a heron waded, fetching breakfast.

"What now?" asked the goat.

"Find the fish," said the horse.

"Bird," said the dog, "do you think that heron may have seen our little friend?"

"He may have," said the bird. "I can ask him. Don't

109

expect too much, though. Herons are notoriously standoffish."

The heron was indeed quite standoffish, and did not

even bother to pick up his head when the bird addressed him.

"What do you want?" asked the heron.

"I would like to know if you have seen a brightly colored fish come this way," said the bird.

"No, I haven't seen any such fish," said the heron. "And if I had I would have eaten it."

"That's not a very nice thing to say," said the bird.

"Tough toads," said the heron.

"Do you know anyone who may have seen the fish?" asked the bird.

"Ask the frogs," said the heron. "I wouldn't mind asking a frog or two some questions myself, if you get my meaning. Now go away, I'm busy!"

"Where might I find the frogs?" asked the bird.

"In the marsh, featherhead!" said the heron. "Where else would you find the tasty little things? Honestly, some birds..."

"Thank you," said the bird. "And tough toads to you too, newt neck!"

Back on the grassy bank, the bird reported to her companions.

"You called the heron a newt neck?" said the cat.

"He called me a featherhead!" said the bird. "And 'newt neck' was all I could think of at the time."

"It isn't important," said the horse. "What is important is that we find this marsh and find the fish in it and be on our way back home."

"Hear! Hear!" the animals cried, and they set off down the river to find the marsh.

They found the marsh sooner than they liked. The dog discovered it first, or rather her nose did. Her nose detected a strong sulfurous smell. It was the smell of rotten eggs and rotten vegetables. It was the stink of acres of decay, and soon the other animals smelled it too. It made their ears ring and their eyes water. It smelled worse than the barn had last summer, when Tom and Troy let two weeks go by without shoveling out the stalls.

Soon after the smell hit them, the ground underfoot turned soft and spongy. With one wrong step off the trail, the horse sank up to his fetlock in thick, black, gunky muck. Out of the muck came clouds of insects—mosquitoes and black flies, gnats and no-see-ums—that hung about the animals' heads in puffs of buzzing, biting smoke.

Out of the muck grew cattails, some higher than the horse's head. Sometimes the trail wandered in among the cattails, and their broken stalks littered the path. They were sharp and painful to walk upon.

"My!" said the horse. "It certainly is noisome in here, isn't it?"

"I don't hear a thing," said the goat, "except for those buzzing bugs."

"Noisome doesn't mean noisy," said the dog. "It means smelly, and I quite agree."

"Oh," said the goat. "Me too."

"A most noisome goo!" said the bird.

"When do you think we will meet up with some frogs, turtle?" asked the dog.

"I was hoping to have met some by now," said the turtle, "but I haven't seen any. Have you, cat?"

"No," said the cat.

"Have you, bird?" asked the turtle.

"Not a one," said the bird.

"Then I'm afraid we shall have to wait until evening," said the turtle.

"Evening!" said the cat. "And spend the night in this awful place? You can't be serious, turtle. There must be some frogs about in this muck! A smelly old marsh is no place for a clean cat to spend the night."

"Oh, hush up, cat!" said the bird. "If you hadn't eaten the fish in the first place we wouldn't be wandering about in this dreadful place!"

"I did not eat the fish," said the cat. "But I may very well eat you!"

And with that the cat took a swipe at the bird with her paw. It was not a very serious swipe, but nevertheless the bird flew up in a flutter from her perch on the dog's rump. She flew high up in the air and then dove down on the cat all in a rush, turning her sharp beak away at the last second. The cat got a feather in her face and took another swipe at the fleeing bird.

"Stop it! Both of you!" said the horse.

The bird made one more mock dive and then came to perch on the horse's head.

"Stop it!" said the horse.

"The cat swiped first!" said the bird.

"I didn't even have my claws out," said the cat.

"Stop!" said the horse. "We started this trip together and we will finish it together. Would you rather spend another night in the pines, cat?"

"No," said the cat.

"Would you, bird?" asked the horse.

"No," said the bird, "but—"

"Then both of you please keep your opinions to yourself," said the horse. "Now, turtle, why must we wait until evening to see some frogs?"

"Because that is when the frogs come out to sing," said the turtle. "And they will come out, believe me.

114

This marsh is a frog paradise."

"Some paradise," said the cat.

"Oh, shut up, cat!" said the bird.

"A rather nose-some paradise, I think," said the goat.

"That's noisome, goat," said the dog. "Noisome."

In the middle of the wet cattail marsh was a shallow pool, and in the middle of the shallow pool was a small, dry island. In the middle of the small dry island was an old, gnarled red maple tree.

It was a wet crossing. The cold water came up to the goat's chest, and halfway across, his hoof struck something slimy in the muck.

"Ick," said the goat. "What happened to the river, dog? I liked it much better than this."

"It's all around us," said the dog, who swam beside the goat.

The cat could not swim across, so she hitched a ride on the horse's back, along with the spider and the turtle. The turtle could have swum across, but he didn't want to show off. Riding on the horse's back was much quicker, anyway. The bird didn't mind showing off in the least, and she flew from the path to the island and back again seven times before the others arrived.

The bird flew from the path to the island and back
again seven times before the others arrived.

The animals sat on the island under the red maple and waited for evening to come, when they could have an audience with the frogs. They waited and waited and waited. They waited as the sun climbed and sank and as their shadows went from long to short to long again.

The dog and the cat slept for the most part, arising only occasionally to turn about and then settle back to sleep. The horse slept some of the time and spent the rest of the time swatting insects with his long tail. The bird and the turtle chatted about places they had been to and places they might go. The spider and the goat passed the time by counting snakes. By the day's end the spider had counted twenty-three snakes and the goat had counted ten. The goat had seen more than ten snakes, but ten was as high as he could count.

"Well, turtle," said the bird, "the sun is setting and I still don't see any frogs."

"Half a moment," said the turtle.

"Be patient, bird," said the horse, "and have confidence in the turtle. Without his expertise we would never have been able to get even this far."

"Thank you, horse," said the turtle.

117

"Don't mention it," said the horse.

"Oh, I didn't mean anything by it," said the bird. "I'm just so impatient with this smelly old marsh. I wish I was home in my dry little nest."

"We all wish we were home," said the horse. "And the sooner we find the fish, the sooner we will be."

"In any case, bird," said the turtle, "we will hear the frogs before we see them, if we see any at all."

"I do wish the sun would hurry up and set!" said the bird.

The sun was then a bright red disk, and half of it had already disappeared below the horizon. The tops of the cattails seemed on fire in its light.

"Come out, frogs!" sang the bird. "Come out, come out, wherever you are!"

"I do wish you would shut up," said the cat.

"Hush," said the turtle.

The last red speck of the sun sank and evening fell. The fiery light was gone from the tops of the cattails, and stars had already appeared in the darkening eastern sky. A moment passed, and then another, and then the whole marsh erupted in a roar of sound.

"CROAK CROAK CROAK CROAK CROAK CROAK!"

"What did I tell you?" said the turtle.

118

"Oh, my!" said the bird.

"CROAK CROAK CROAK CROAK CROAK CROAK CROAK!"

"Oh, marsh full of frogs!" said the turtle, as loud as his leathery voice allowed. "I am a turtle looking for a little lost fish, a brightly colored little fish, with colors that shift and shimmer as she swims about!"

"CROAK CROAK CROAK!" sang the frogs.

"Have you seen such a fish?" asked the turtle.

All was quiet for a moment, and then a reply came.

"MAYBE MAYBE MAYBE," sang the frogs.

"You have!" said the turtle.

"MAYBE MAYBE MAYBE," sang the frogs.

"Have you seen her recently?" asked the turtle.

"MAYBE MAYBE MAYBE," sang the frogs.

"Is this fish among you now?" asked the turtle.

"MAYBE NOT MAYBE NOT," sang the frogs.

"Is the fish farther

upstream?" asked the turtle.

"MAYBE NOT MAYBE NOT," sang the frogs.

"Is the fish farther downstream?" asked the turtle.

"MAYBE MAYBE MAYBE," sang the frogs.

"Much farther downstream?" asked the turtle.

"MAYBE NOT MAYBE NOT MAYBE NOT," sang the frogs.

"What is all this 'maybe' and 'maybe not' business?" asked the bird, who understood something of the frog language.

"It's just the way frogs are," said the turtle.

"Do they know or don't they?" the bird asked.

"MAYBE, MAYBE NOT," sang the frogs.

"I just want to know whether it is 'yes' or 'no'!" said the bird. "The salamander said 'yes.' The bear said 'no.' The trout said 'yes.' The heron said—"

"No, bird!" said the turtle. "Don't say that!"

But it was too late. With the mention of the word 'heron,' the frogs shut up and shut up for good. They

120

answered no more of the turtle's questions and sang not a note more that night.

"Don't you know not to mention herons when talking to frogs?" asked the turtle.

"I just didn't think of it, turtle," said the bird. "I'm so sorry. Now I've ruined everything."

"Why can't you say 'heron' to a frog?" whispered the spider to the dog.

"It's like saying 'spider' to a fly," said the dog.

"Oh."

"Won't the frogs come back, turtle?" asked the horse.

"I think not," said the turtle. "They are down deep in the muck right now, and I don't think they'll come up again until we are gone."

"I'm sorry!" said the bird.

"It can't be helped," said the turtle. "I didn't have much more to say to them anyway. We do know that the fish has been seen recently downstream, and not much farther downstream at that. All is not lost."

"I am so sorry," said the bird. "I should have thought before I spoke. But I've never met such indecisive creatures in all my life!"

"Oh, bird!" said the cat. "You really are a featherhead."

The animals spent the remainder of the evening

camped out under the old red maple on the island in the cattail sea. The horse and the goat and the spider and the bird and the turtle went to sleep. The cat and the dog, however, had slept all day, and they stayed up to watch the moon rise. Back at the large house they often passed the long nights together. On this night, the moon was only a night away from being full, and its pale light cast faint shadows about the marsh.

"It's quite beautiful, isn't it?" said the dog.

"The moon, do you mean?" asked the cat.

"Yes," said the dog. "The night isn't so frightening when the moon is out."

"You find the night frightening?" asked the cat.

"Sometimes I do," said the dog. "When I can smell things but can't see them. Doesn't the night sometimes frighten you?"

"Not the night itself," said the cat. "I can see through the night."

"I wish I could see through the night," said the dog.

"You can smell through it," said the cat.

"I suppose so," said the dog.

An owl on the prowl flew across the marsh, and they watched its silhouette pass in front of the moon.

"What does frighten you, cat?" asked the dog.

122

"The water frightens me," said the cat. "The piney wood frightens me. I was frightened of you when we first met."

"You certainly had a strange way of showing it," said the dog. "You scratched my nose, if I recall."

"I was just a kitten then," said the cat.

"I remember," said the dog.

"Think how frightened the fish must be," said the cat, "all alone out there in that water somewhere."

"Yes," said the dog. "But I'll bet my best bone we find her soon."

"I hope you're right," said the cat. "This river seems to go on and on, and we with it."

"It must have an end somewhere," said the dog.

"Why?" asked the cat.

"It had a beginning, so it must have an ending," said the dog.

"I suppose so," said the cat.

They sat for a while under the old red maple on the island in the cattail sea, watching the moon rise.

"Dog," said the cat, "do you think the moon is really made of cream?"

After the Animals

It was not until the day after the meeting in the hayloft that the grown-ups of the large house discovered the truth about the mysterious mystery of the missing pets. And although Tim, Tom, Tod, Tad, Ted, Troy, William, and Lillian would have liked you to believe that they revealed the truth about the mystery willingly, it wasn't quite so. Rather, the truth about the mysterious mystery of the missing pets came out by accident.

The accident happened during dinner, during that quiet time in the meal when everyone's belly is almost full and worrisome thoughts are a long way off. Then their mom asked a question, and worrisome thoughts came hurrying back.

"I haven't seen the cat recently," she said. "And she hasn't touched her food in days. I wonder where she could be. Have you seen her at all, Tod?"

"No, Mom," Tod said, and began to eat his green beans, which he really did not like.

"That's funny," their dad said. "I haven't seen the dog around lately. Have you seen her, Tim?"

"No, Dad," Tim said. Tim had already finished his green beans, so he ate his mashed potatoes instead.

"Isn't that strange," said Uncle Nat. "I was out in the barn today, and I could not find hide nor hair of the horse or the goat. Have you seen them, Troy and Tom?"

"No, Uncle Nat," said Troy and Tom.

"Well, what do you know!" said Aunt Alice. "I went out to the maple grove yesterday to give the bird some suet I had left over from my pie filling—you know, I used to use the leftovers for suet pudding but since old Mr. Moonmorrow passed away no one around here will eat suet pudding, not even you, Nat—and so I went to give it to the bird but the bird wasn't there! I thought she might be with the turtle, so I went down to the stream, but wouldn't you know, the turtle did not seem to be about, either! Have you seen them, boys?"

"No, Aunt Alice," said Tad and Ted.

It was all too much for William. Tim, Tom, Tod, Tad, Ted, and Troy had gotten off easy. Their secrets were out. No one had asked him anything about the spider yet, but they certainly would, and what was he going to say? William had eaten up all his green beans and mashed potatoes, so he drank his milk, which was really

126

too warm at that point to drink comfortably. With each gulp he sank down lower in his seat, and when he was done he even wiped away his milk mustache.

"William?" his mother said.

William's face turned pink. Perhaps he could pretend he hadn't heard her.

"William?" his mother repeated.

William's face turned red. This was all too much to take!

"William?" she said.

"The spider is missing, too!" he blurted out. "All the animals are missing!"

"What?" his father said.

"Missing, you say?" Uncle Nat said.

"Oh, my stars!" said Aunt Alice.

"William," his mother said, "I was just going to ask you to please pass the bread."

"Yes, Mom," William said, handing her the bread basket, but it was too late. The tale was out.

Telling their mom and dad about the missing animals was not so bad as the seven brothers thought it would be. Worrying about a thing is almost always worse than the thing itself, and in the end the brothers were quite relieved that the news was out.

Mom and Dad and Uncle Nat and Aunt Alice were not angry about the missing animals, they were concerned. They were angry, however, about receiving the news three days late. But then Tim explained that they had been meeting in the hayloft, trying to decide what to do.

"And we decided that the other animals went looking for the missing fish," said Tom.

"And we decided that the place the fish was probably missing was the creek in the pasture," said Tod.

"So we thought we would follow the creek downstream," said Tad, "and find the animals and the fish."

Mom and Dad were still a little angry with Lillian and their seven sons, but they saw that their search plan was a good one. Dad said he would help them carry the three canoes down to the creek in the pasture in the morning. Mom said she would pack lunches for Tim, Tom, Tod, Tad, Ted, Troy, William, and Lillian in case they became hungry paddling, as they surely would.

"How far down the creek do you think you'll go?" asked Uncle Nat.

"At least as far as the marsh," said Tim. "And

maybe all the way to the lake. It shouldn't take that long. We'll be back before supper."

"You had better be," Mom said. "But take a flashlight, just in case."

"There's a beaver dam below the marsh now," said Uncle Nat. "Your father and I were back in there last spring."

"That's right," Dad said. "I imagine that beaver dam is pretty big now."

"I bet you're right," Uncle Nat said.

"Maybe we should go along with Lillian and the boys," Dad said. "What do you think, Nat?"

"Oh, no!" Aunt Alice said. "Let the children go alone. The animals are their responsibilities. Besides, there are only three canoes, and with the weight you've put on lately, Nat, you would need one all to yourself!"

Early the next morning Tim, Tom, Tod, Tad, Ted, Troy, William, and Lillian set off downstream from the pasture behind the barn. Tim, Ted, and William were in the first boat. Tod, Troy, and Lillian were in the second. Tom and Tad were in the last. They carried eight box lunches, six pocket knives, four wax pencils, three flashlights, two compasses, one map, and one dead fly. The dead fly was William's, and he kept it in his pocket.

The End of the River

Early the next morning the animals arose and once again made the wet crossing from the island back to the path. Although their bodies were rested, their minds were not, and they were not a very cheerful crew. For one thing, the marsh water was cold on their coats, and the sun was still too low in the sky to warm them. For another, the path seemed to go on and on, with no end in sight.

"It seems as if we are always almost and never quite there," said the goat. "How much farther must we go?"

"Things do seem forlorn," said the horse, "but we must press on."

The goat did not know what "forlorn" meant, but this morning he did not even care.

"Why must we press on?" asked the bird. "We've been after the fish four whole days now and we still haven't found her. What makes you think we ever will? I for one am not willing to spend the rest of my days looking for a little lost fish. I've got better things to do."

"Now you're making sense," said the cat.

"At least we agree on something, cat," said the bird. "I

tell you, I'm of half a mind to fly back home right now!"

"I wish I had wings," said the spider.

"You may return if you want to, bird," said the turtle. "But I am going to continue."

"As am I," said the horse.

"Oh, I'm not going anywhere, except with you," said the bird. "I am just tired of this journey, tired of the muck and mire, tired of stupid frogs that don't know yes from no, tired of insolent herons, and tired of the dark pinewood and terrible things that frighten you in the night. And I just don't know if we will ever find the fish. I just don't know."

The bird's words rang true. The thought that the fish would never be found was a thought all the animals shared, and they all began to have doubts: doubts that the little fish would ever be found, and doubts that their search served any purpose.

All except the dog, that is. The dog seemed completely untroubled. She walked with a spring in her step and a wag in her tail, wandering to and fro in the cool morning air. Sometimes she wandered off to the left of the trail, and sometimes to the right, and sometimes she would bound ahead of the rest and then wait patiently for them to catch up. And if her head hung low, it was only to sniff the ground with her keen nose.

By midmorning the trail was drier and the cattail marsh had been left behind. The path passed through an abandoned farm field, a melancholy place. An old stone wall covered by vines ran partway along the edge of the field. The path passed through this wall in a spot where the stones had tumbled out. Where the well of the farm had been was now a dark, stony hole in the ground. Where the house had been was now only a stony cellar, open to the sky,

133

with pools of stagnant water in the bottom. A faded wagon track led away to the west.

A few stray pines grew in clumps about the field. There were not many clumps, and the trees were not very tall, but these young pines served as a grim reminder of the animals' recent journey through the dark forest, a journey they would have to undertake again if they were ever to return home.

"Will our large house ever look like this?" asked the goat.

"Someday, perhaps," said the horse. "But not while Lillian and her seven brothers are about."

"I hope not," said the goat.

At the far end of the field the trail passed through a poplar thicket. Many of the poplars had gnaw marks in their bark. Some of them had been gnawed clean through and dragged off, so that only a stump with a pointed top remained.

"What kind of beast eats trees?" asked the horse. "This is very strange."

"Woodpeckers bore holes in trees," said the bird, "but I've never met one that actually ate them."

"I think I know who did this," said the turtle. "We shall soon see."

And they did soon see. The river began to widen, and the waters became flat and still, and a gentle trickle could be heard. After the next bend in the trail the river widened still more and became a pond. At the end of the pond was a dam made of mud and beech wood. In the middle of the pond was a round mound of beech wood that stuck up a few feet above the level of the water.

"What's all this?" asked the horse.

"Is it part of the old farm?" asked the goat.

"No," said the turtle. "It's a beaver pond. And that is a beaver dam. And that is a beaver lodge."

"Is the fish in here?" asked the spider.

"She could be," said the turtle. "I'll walk out on the dam to where the water spills over and nose around. I think if she is in here the current will have carried her near the spillway."

"What if she spilled over?" asked the goat.

"She may very well have," said the turtle. "Dog, do you think you and the bird could go down the trail a ways, and see what becomes of the water? If you meet any river creatures and you can speak to them, ask them if they have seen the fish. Perhaps we can narrow down her whereabouts. The frogs said she was not far

135

downstream, and I happen to believe them, even if others among us do not."

"All right, turtle," said the dog. "Are you coming, bird?"

"I'm coming!" said the bird with a ruffle of her feathers. "But I still don't think the frogs knew what they were talking about!"

The bird and the dog set off down the trail. They passed the beaver dam and the spillway and disappeared around a bend in the river. While they were gone the turtle made his way out to the middle of the dam where the water spilled over. He walked at a turtle's pace, however, and just as he got to the spillway he heard shouts behind him.

The dog and the bird had returned from their scouting expedition and were standing with the other animals at the spot where the beaver dam met the shore. They were shouting at the turtle, but the turtle could not make out their words over the sound of the spillway. At last the bird flew out and perched next to the turtle.

"Turtle!" said the bird. "We've found the end of the river, the end of the river!"

"What do you mean, the end of the river?" asked

the turtle. "Rivers have no end, except at the sea. Do you mean you've come across the sea?"

"Not the sea," said the bird, "but it might as well be. It's a lake! A gigantic lake!"

"Oh, my!" said the turtle, and he hurried off the dam as fast as his little legs could carry him.

The Turtle Makes a Discovery

W e went around one bend, and then another," said the dog, "and then the river opened up into a wide, wide lake. It's wider than any water I have ever seen, turtle."

"Oh, my!" said the turtle.

"It would take a day to walk to the end of it," said the dog. "And three days to walk around it."

"Oh, my," said the turtle.

"I don't know how many days it would take you to swim it, turtle," said the dog. "If you could swim it at all."

"This is most terrible news!" said the turtle.

"I'm very sorry," said the dog. "Very, very sorry."

"And you weren't able to speak to anyone?" asked the turtle.

"We saw a pair of loons out in the middle the lake," said the bird. "But it would be pointless to talk to them."

"I suppose you're right," said the turtle. "And I suppose we have reached the end."

"The end?" asked the cat. "What do you mean, turtle?"

"The end of the river," said the turtle. "The end of our journey. The end of our search for the little lost fish."

"Oh, no!" said the goat.

"Oh, yes," said the turtle. "I'm afraid so."

"Can't something be done?" asked the horse. "Can't we at least take a look around the lake?"

"You have to see the lake for yourself, horse," said the dog. "It makes this beaver pond look like a puddle."

"The lake could hold a hundred thousand of our little lost fish," said the turtle. "And it would take forever to find her, if she is still to be found."

"What do you mean?" asked the spider.

"There are other things besides herons that like to eat fish," said the turtle. "There are other birds and other beasts. And worst of all, other fish. Bass and pike and muskellunge, walleye and lake trout. Fish to which our little one would be but a mouthful. If the little lost fish is in the lake, I'm afraid we shall never find her."

"But we must!" said the goat. "We must!"

"The little fish has passed into the wide world," said the turtle. "There is nothing we can do except follow her and risk getting lost ourselves."

These last words were too much for the goat, and he burst into tears.

140

"We must," he muttered. "We must."

"There now," said the horse, and the goat nuzzled his nose into the horse's side.

The other animals fell silent, each thinking thoughts about the little lost fish.

"It seems too cruel to have come all this way and fail," said the bird.

"But we have failed," said the horse. "We have come all this way to find the little lost fish, and we have failed. This is a very sad day."

"Poor little fish!" said the dog.

"Through thistle fields and the pinewood and a smelly old marsh," said the bird. "Whipped by spruce trees, cut by thorns, almost eaten by a big black beast. And all for nothing. For nothing at all."

"And to think we began this journey because we were afraid of the new pet Lillian would get!" said the horse. "I would gladly share my stall with a dozen colts if only the little lost fish could be found."

"And I would share my web with a dozen other spiders," said the spider.

"And I would share my creek with a dozen turtles," said the turtle.

"Poor little fish!" said the dog.

All the animals fell silent, thinking of the little lost fish.

"I suppose you can take your collar off now, cat," said the horse. "I think we would all agree, even the bird, that you are innocent."

"It's true," said the bird. "I no longer believe you ate the fish, and I'm sorry for ever thinking so."

"Thank you, bird," said the cat. "Thank you all. But I think I'll keep the collar on for awhile, if just in memory of the little lost fish."

"We shall all remember her," said the spider.

The horse took in a bushelful of air and let it out in a long, low, mournful whinny.

"We must return home now," he said. "We have done all we could, and unfortunately it has not been enough. But I imagine that Tim, Tom, Tod, Tad, Ted, Troy, and William are worried about us, and it would not be fair to delay any longer."

So the animals prepared for the journey home. It was just noon and time for lunch. The horse and the goat moved away from the beaver dam and grazed on some grass that grew beside the path.

"I'm not at all hungry," said the goat.

"You must eat something," said the horse. "It is a long journey home, and you will need nourishment."

142

"All right," said the goat. "But I'm not at all hungry, and I don't think I ever shall be again."

The bird fluttered about the woods and dug up some grubs beside a fallen log.

"I ought to be singing!" she said to herself. "Singing a song of going home."

The bird blew a few notes through her beak, but soon stopped short.

"It's no good," she said. "That's a happy song, and I'm not happy. The only song I feel like singing is a song about the little lost fish, but that's a song with too sad an ending."

The spider hopped up into a poplar tree and strung his web. He strung a string from branch to branch and strung a strand from string to string.

"What good have I been on this trip?" the spider asked himself. "I can't lead like the horse. I can't keep the trail like the dog. I can't talk to the river creatures like the turtle. All I can do is spin webs and catch flies. If only I could spin a net and catch the little lost fish!"

The cat and the dog went off into the thicket.

"At least the return journey will go much more quickly," said the cat. "There won't be any need to stop and make inquiries about the fish."

"Yes," said the dog.

"It's strange, though," said the cat. "Ever since we passed through the pinewood I've been looking forward to going back home. But now that we are actually returning I am not happy at all."

"I know what you mean," said the dog. "And I was so sure that we would find the fish! My nose has never failed me up till now. I must be getting old. I suppose I'll have to spend the rest of my days on the rug by the stove."

"Don't say such a thing," said the cat. "We all make mistakes."

The turtle wandered off towards the edge of the beaver pond. He walked even slower than usual, filled with a great sadness about the missing fish and feeling a failure as an ambassador.

"Was there some creature I did not talk to that I should have?" he asked himself. "Was there some question I forgot to ask?"

He came to the water's edge. On his way across the beaver dam he had noticed some very tasty waterweeds that were difficult to find around the creek in the maple grove, and this was what he had come to the pond's edge to eat.

144

"In my younger days I would have gone far out of my way for a bite of meat," the turtle said, "but lately I prefer to eat nothing but greens. I wonder what the little lost fish eats, out in the wide world. If something in the wide world hasn't already eaten her. Poor little fish!"

He nibbled at the top of the weed and then moved down the tender stalk. "A very tasty weed," he said, "and I wager that the wet part is the tastiest of all."

He stuck his head underwater to nibble there.

And then something caught his eye. A streak of bright colors flashed among the weeds. The turtle stopped chewing and stared about, but nothing could be seen. It must be the sunshine, the turtle thought, filtering through the pond water. He went back to nibbling.

But there it was again! A streak of bright colors, colors that seemed to shift and shimmer among the weed stalks. The turtle stopped chewing and stared about, but nothing could be seen. It must be some colorful leaves that have fallen into the pond, the turtle thought, although it was a little early in the year for leaves to be falling. He went back to nibbling, but this time he kept his head up and his eyes wide open.

There it was again! These colors were alive.

Whatever it was, it certainly wasn't leaves, and it certainly wasn't light. Could it be? No, it couldn't be. Still, there was no harm in asking. The turtle swallowed his food and spoke.

"Fish?" he said. "Is that you, fish?"

Nothing moved for a moment, and then a rainbow-colored head poked out of the weeds. It was a fish head, attached to a fish body, with a fish tail and fins!

"Fish!" said the turtle. "Is that you?"

"Turtle?" said the fish head. "Is that you?"

"It is," said the turtle.

"Then I'm me!" said the fish, for she was indeed the fish—the little lost fish they had come so far to find.

"Oh, my!" said the turtle. "Oh my oh my oh my!"

"I am not dreaming, am I?" asked the fish.

"No," said the turtle. "Not unless I am too, and I'm quite sure I'm not."

"But what are you doing here, turtle?" asked the fish. "Surely you didn't get washed downstream too?"

"Oh, my! Oh, my!" said the turtle. "So that is what happened. We thought so. We thought as much. Oh, my!"

"We?" asked the fish.

"Yes!" said the turtle. "The horse and the goat and

146

A rainbow-colored head poked out of the weeds.

the dog and the bird and the spider and the cat and I! We all came to look for you, and now you are found. Stay right where you are, and I'll fetch the others."

And now it was the fish's turn to say, "Oh, my!"

The turtle scrambled up the bank of the pond and moved as quickly as he could towards the path, where the horse and goat stood grazing.

"I've found her!" shouted the turtle. "Or rather she's found me! Or one or the other, oh my!"

"Found who, turtle?" asked the horse. "What are you talking about? Are you quite all right?"

"Yes," said the turtle. "I am fine. The fish! I've found the fish, horse. The fish!"

"Are you sure?" asked the horse. The horse could not believe it was true, and did not want to get his hopes up just to have them dashed.

"Quite sure," said the turtle. "Quite, quite sure. Come look for yourself, and bring the others!"

Soon the horse and the goat and the cat and the dog and the spider and the bird were all gathered on the pond's edge, around where the waterweeds grew. They peered into the water, but it was difficult to see anything past the glare of the sun. The turtle pulled his head out of the water.

148

"Where is she, turtle?" asked the goat.

"I can't see anything," said the spider.

"Are you sure she is in there?" asked the cat.

"Say hello to her for us, won't you?" said the bird.

"I already have said hello," said the turtle. "And the fish has informed me that she wishes to say hello to you, in her own way, of course."

Then there was a shimmer on the surface of the pond, and the little fish leapt clear of the water and did three somersaults in the air, and then landed with a big splash. She was a beautiful fish, with all the colors of the rainbow on her body, colors that seemed to shift and shimmer in the sunlight. She was a little fish, but she was no longer lost.

"Hooray!" they all shouted. "Hooray! Hooray! The little fish is found!"

The animals were so happy that the fish had been found that they began to dance. The dog danced with the cat. The horse danced with the goat. The bird danced with the turtle (which was quite a sight to see). The spider danced by himself on the end of a silken string, and the fish turned somersaults above the surface of the water.

They had no music to dance to, so the animals made

their own music. The horse neighed, the dog barked, the cat meowed, and the bird sang. The goat bleated, the fish splashed, the spider plucked silk, and the turtle drummed on his shell. They danced and drummed and splashed and bleated. They sang and meowed and barked and neighed. They made such a racket that they woke the beavers, and the beavers came out of their lodge to see what was going on.

A Reunion

W hat was that?" said Tim.

Tim, Tom, Tod, Tad, Ted, Troy, William, and Lillian had just finished lunch. They had stopped to eat on the small island in the small pond in the cattail marsh, and were resting with their backs against the old red maple.

"What was what?" said Tom.

"I thought I heard a dog bark," said Tim. "I thought I heard *the* dog bark."

Lillian and the seven brothers sat still and listened.

"I hear something, " said Tom. "But it isn't a dog barking, it's a horse neighing. And I think it's *the* horse."

Lillian and the seven brothers sat still and listened.

"That's no horse!" said Tod. "That's a cat meowing. And it sounds like *the* cat!"

Lillian and the seven brothers listened once again.

"Cat!" said Ted. "Phooey! That's a bird singing if it's anything, and I think it's *the* bird."

Lillian and the seven brothers sat and listened for a moment longer, and then Tad stood up.

"C'mon!" he shouted. "What are we waiting for?"

Quick as a wink, and almost as quick as they had unpacked them, Tim, Tom, Tod, Tad, Ted, Troy, William, and Lillian packed up their lunches and stowed them in the canoes. When all the crumpled napkins and apple cores and tin drinking cups were accounted for, they shoved off the island and paddled furiously downstream.

They paddled hard, with deep, long strokes. They paddled so hard that the bow of each boat seemed to rise up out of the water. They paddled so hard that the wake of the canoes became waves that lapped against the banks of the river. They paddled so hard that William and Lillian thought they were in a race, and when the boat William was in passed the boat Lillian was in, he stuck his tongue out at her.

They paddled so hard that they soon paddled out of the cattail marsh. They paddled past the old abandoned farm with its open cellar and collapsed well and overgrown stone wall. They paddled past the beech wood thicket with its chewed-off stumps. They paddled around a bend in the river and into the beaver pond, and there they saw a peculiar sight.

"It's the dog!" said Tim.

"It's the bird!" said Ted.

"It's the spider!" said William.

Tim, Ted, and William were in the first boat to arrive in the pond, and Tom and Tad soon arrived in the second.

"It's the horse!" said Tom.

"It's the turtle!" said Tad.

Tod, Troy, and Lillian were in the last boat.

"It's the cat!" said Tod.

"It's the goat!" said Troy.

Lillian held her hand against her forehead to shade her eyes from the sun. She looked for a long time toward the bank where the animals stood, but she could see no sign of her little lost fish. She leaned over the gunwale of the canoe and looked into the cool, dark depths. But the glare was too bright, and all that she saw there was her own reflection.

Then a ripple broke the surface of the pond, and something leapt into the air, something bright and colorful, with all the colors of the rainbow on its body, colors that seemed to shift and shimmer in the strong sunlight. Something that did three somersaults, and then landed on the surface with a big splash.

"It's the fish!" shouted Lillian. "My little found fish!"

"Hooray!" shouted Tim, Tom, and Tod.

"Yippee!" shouted Tad, Ted, and Troy.

"Oops," said William, for at that moment the canoe he was standing in started forward, and he fell headfirst into the beaver pond. It is never a very good idea to stand up in a canoe, but fortunately William had a life jacket on, and the pond at that spot was not very deep. Tim, Tom, Tod, Tad, Ted, and Troy soon had the canoes and the soaking-wet William ashore.

"Hello, dog!" said Tim.

The dog barked and wagged her tail.

"Hello, horse!" said Tom.

The horse whinnied and pranced about.

"Hello, cat!" said Tod.

The cat purred and rubbed against Tod's leg.

"Hello, turtle!" said Tad.

The turtle kept his leathery legs and head outside his shell instead of closing himself up, which was his way of saying he was happy.

"Hello, bird!" said Ted.

The bird sang and perched on Ted's finger.

"Hello, goat!" said Troy.

The goat bleated and gave Troy a gentle nudge.

"Hi, spider," said William. "I brought a fly for you. Only now it's all wet."

The little fish leapt high into the air and turned somersaults, happy to be found.

The spider took the fly anyway, and danced on her eight little legs.

"Hello, fish!" said Lillian, who knelt at the water's edge. "I'm so happy you're no longer lost!"

The little fish leapt high into the air and turned somersaults, happy to be found.

After each of the seven brothers had said hello to each of their particular pets, they went around and said hello to all the other animals. They had not seen each other for some days, and it was quite a reunion. Lillian went around to all the others too, thanking

each pet individually for finding the little fish. She brushed the horse, butted the goat, scratched the dog, petted the cat, sang to the bird, bowed to the spider, and rubbed the turtle's shell.

"Well," said Tim. "We have found the animals, and the animals have found the fish. But if we don't start back now, we won't find any dinner on the table, so let's get going."

"Give me a hand with the saddle, Troy," said Tom.

Troy and Tom lifted the saddle out of the canoe, along with a bridle and a blanket and a long rope. The

saddle and saddlecloth and bridle went on the horse, and the rope went around the goat. Then Tom hopped in the saddle.

"I'm going to turn at the abandoned farm," he said. "Down the cart track and up the old town road. Last one home doesn't get any cake!"

Tom rode away up the path, pulling the goat behind him.

"Okay, everybody," said Tod. "Let's go!"

"You ride with me, Ted," said Tad.

"And you pick up a paddle, William," said Tim. "With Tom gone we're shorthanded."

William picked up a paddle.

"But I can't paddle very well," he said.

"That's okay," said Tim. "I'll do most of it. Just sit up front and look like you're paddling."

The dog and the spider rode in the boat with Tim and William. The dog liked riding in the canoe. She liked to hang her head over the side and watch the river go by. The spider didn't think much about boat rides one way or the other, except to note that they were much smoother than a ride between the goat's horns. He spent his time spinning a web between two thwarts.

The cat and the fish rode in Tod, Troy, and Lillian's canoe. The cat did not like riding in boats at all, and she spent the whole trip hiding under Tod's seat. The fish was in her little traveling bowl, which Lillian had filled with pond water.

The bird and the turtle rode in Ted and Tad's boat. The bird spent most of her time outside the boat flying around, but occasionally she came down and perched on the prow. The turtle spent his time in the bottom of the canoe, wallowing in the wash and chewing on the waterweed that Tad had thoughtfully picked.

The return journey went rather quickly, even though they were paddling upstream. The animals had barely settled in before the boys had paddled past the abandoned farm, and soon after that they were passing through the marsh. No frogs sang under the bright sun, and the only sound was of the oars dipping into and out of the water. After the marsh came the still stretch of river and the bank of lush green grass.

And then came the pines. The current was faster there, and the boats slowed to a crawl. They crawled past the burnt section of pines with its ominous black trees. They crawled past the grove of rotting hardwoods with its vines and creepers that stretched all the

159

way across the stream. They crawled past the briar patch and its inch-long thorns.

At the rapids the boats were beached on the long, sandy bank and carried above the rough water. The turtle thought he saw the flash of a brook trout fin in the tumbling stream, but he couldn't quite be sure. After the rapids they passed the mouth of the mountain creek, and after the mouth of the mountain creek they passed the clearing where the berry bushes grew, and where the big black bear had come upon them. That night seemed so long ago! Still, it was better to be passing the bushes by in a boat.

The air smelled sweet under the pines, and the canoes rocked gently to and fro as they worked their way upstream, and one by one the animals fell asleep. The dog shut her eyes for just a moment and fell asleep with her head still on the gunwale. The bird tucked her head under her wing for just a moment and fell asleep perched on the prow. The cat fell asleep under the seat, the spider in her web, the turtle in the wash in the bottom of the boat. The fish dozed off in her traveling bowl.

For the first time in days the animals felt safe. For the first time in a long time they felt comfortable (except for the cat, that is, who felt a little seasick). For the first time in many nights they slept peacefully, dreaming only pleasant dreams. When they awoke it was evening, and Lillian and her seven brothers were pulling the canoes out of the stream and into the meadow behind the barn.

Waiting for Spring

The return made everyone in the large house very happy. Tim, Tom, Tod, Tad, Ted, Troy, William, and Lillian were happy to have the animals back. Their mom, dad, Aunt Alice, and Uncle Nat were happy to have Tim, Tom, Tod, Tad, Ted, Troy, William, and Lillian back, even if they were a little late for dinner. And, of course, the animals were happy too.

The rescue of the little fish was the talk of the barnyard for many months. The fame of the seven animals spread far and wide, and they were quite looked up to among others of their kind.

Cats of every color and stripe (even a Siamese) came from miles around to hear the tale firsthand, and collars on cats (without bells, of course) became all the rage that year. Dogs are not allowed to gather in packs unless officially employed, so they came to the large house in ones and twos to see for themselves the nose that sniffed a fish through water.

The horse and the goat spent most afternoons that autumn against the fence in the far pasture, telling and retelling the story of their adventure to the livestock of the Four Corners Farm. They told the Four Corners Sheep seventeen times, and the Four Corners Oxen six times, and the Four Corners Chickens 293 times. Even the Four Corners Cattle, who rarely cared a cud about anything outside the wire, heard the tale twice.

Meanwhile, up north, news of the adventure somehow found its way into the travel brochures, and all that fall the bird's tree was a popular stop on the great migration. One day there was even a flock of geese under the tree, which was quite a waddle from the stock pond.

And although fame may be a fine thing for a cat or a dog or a horse or a bird, it isn't so for a spider. For a spider, the less publicity, the better. Bugs no longer dared to buzz near the eaves of the large house, nor the rafters of the barn, and the spider had to spread his webs far and wide just to catch a decent meal.

Even the turtle found some measure of fame, although not right away. News among turtles spreads slowly, and it was not until the cold weather came, when the boughs of the birches were bent in arcs under the snow, that the full story filtered downstream.

The fish was famous, too, although it hardly mattered. She was just happy to be back. Happy to be back home, safe and sound, swimming back and forth and back and forth (and sometimes even forth and back) in the big tank lined with gravel and rocks and plants that stood at the foot of Lillian's bed.

But as happy as the fish was, she was something else too, something she couldn't quite name or put a fin on. It was a strange and mysterious feeling, and a feeling that grew larger with each passing day, with each twist and turn among the rocks and plants of her little tank.

For as frightening as her journey was, it was very exciting, too, and she missed it. She missed the rough and wild water and all the adventure it could bring.

But summer was over and winter had come, and it would be a long time until the fish was able to return to her little pool in the meadow, until she would feel once more the fine cool water of the stream flowing through her fins. And so she swam back and forth and back and forth (and sometimes even forth and back) in the big tank that stood at the foot of Lillian's bed, waiting for spring.

THE END